D0724155

MORE MYSTERIES FROM THE
BERKLEY PUBLISHING GROUP...

SISTER FREVISSE MYSTERIES: Medieval mystery in the tradition of
Ellis Peters...

by Margaret Frazer

THE NOVICE'S TALE

THE OUTLAW'S TALE

THE PRIORESS' TALE

THE SERVANT'S TALE

THE BISHOP'S TALE

THE BOY'S TALE

THE MURDERER'S TALE

THE MAIDEN'S TALE

THE REEVE'S TALE

THE SQUIRE'S TALE

PENNYFOOT HOTEL MYSTERIES: In Edwardian England, death takes
a seaside holiday...

by Kate Kingsbury

ROOM WITH A CLUE

SERVICE FOR TWO

CHECK-OUT TIME

DEATH WITH RESERVATIONS

DO NOT DISTURB

EAT, DRINK, AND BE BURIED

GROUNDS FOR MURDER

PAY THE PIPER

CHIVALRY IS DEAD

RING FOR TOMB SERVICE

MAID TO MURDER

GLYNIS TRYON MYSTERIES: The highly acclaimed series set in the
early days of the women's rights movement...
"Historically accurate and telling."—Sara Paretsky

by Miriam Grace Monfredo

SENECA FALLS INHERITANCE

BLACKWATER SPIRITS

NORTH STAR CONSPIRACY

THROUGH A GOLD EAGLE

THE STALKING-HORSE

MUST THE MAIDEN DIE

SISTERS OF CAIN

BROTHERS OF CAIN

MARK TWAIN MYSTERIES: "Adventurous...Replete with genuine
tall tales from the great man himself."—*Mostly Murder*

by Peter J. Heck

DEATH ON THE MISSISSIPPI

A CONNECTICUT YANKEE IN CRIMINAL COURT

THE PRINCE AND THE PROSECUTOR

THE GUILTY ABROAD

THE MYSTERIOUS STRANGLER

TOM'S LAWYER

KAREN ROSE CERCONE: A stunning new historical mystery series
featuring Detective Milo Kachigan and social worker Helen Sorby...

STEEL ASHES

BLOOD TRACKS

COAL BONES

FOR WHOM
DEATH TOLLS

KATE KINGSBURY

BERKLEY PRIME CRIME, NEW YORK

FOR WHOM DEATH TOLLS

A Berkley Prime Crime Book / published by arrangement with the author

PRINTING HISTORY
Berkley Prime Crime mass-market edition / February 2002

Visit our website at
www.penguinputnam.com

ISBN: 0-425-18386-6

Berkley Prime Crime Books are published
by The Berkley Publishing Group,
a division of Penguin Putnam Inc.,
375 Hudson Street, New York, New York 10014.
The name BERKLEY PRIME CRIME and the BERKLEY PRIME CRIME
design are trademarks belonging to Penguin Putnam Inc.

PRINTED IN THE UNITED STATES OF AMERICA

10 9 8 7 6 5 4 3 2 1

CHAPTER

1

"Cricket?" Violet smacked a plate down on the kitchen table with such vehemence, the knives and forks rattled. "What in blue blazes do a bunch of Americans know about playing cricket?"

"Not much, I'm afraid." Lady Elizabeth Hartleigh Compton stared at the pile of bacon, sausages, and scrambled eggs steaming on her plate. For a moment the blissful aroma made her light-headed. "Violet, how on earth did you manage all this? Didn't we use up our ration of eggs this week?"

Violet grunted and moved back to the stove. "Just because there's a bloody war on doesn't mean we have to starve."

"Yes, but—"

"You'd better start eating if you don't want it to get cold."

Elizabeth obediently picked up her knife and fork. She

1

knew that dismissive tone well enough not to argue with her housekeeper. Violet had been with the Hartleigh family since Elizabeth was a child. Sometimes it was hard to ignore that note of authority. There were times when Elizabeth felt as if their positions were reversed, and she was the one obeying orders. Fortunately she considered Violet a dear and trusted friend, one of only two employees left since the good old days when her parents were still alive and a dozen or more servants bustled around the Manor House.

These days no one bustled. Especially Martin, the aging butler, who at that moment was standing in the doorway of the spacious kitchen, sniffing the air like a curious bloodhound.

"Great heavens," he muttered, "it smells like a seaside café in here."

Violet glared at him. "I don't want none of your lip, either, Martin, so sit down and shut up."

Martin lowered his chin and peered over the top of his glasses at Elizabeth. "Good morning, madam. I trust you are feeling well?"

Elizabeth smiled fondly at him. "Quite well, Martin, thank you."

Martin approached the table at his usual snail's pace. "May I have your permission to join you at the table, madam?"

"Of course you may, Martin."

"Thank you, madam."

"Not at all, Martin."

Elizabeth waited for her butler to arrange himself on his chair. The maneuver took a full minute or two. He had barely settled himself before Violet slammed a plate in front of him.

"There," she muttered. "Get that lot down you."

Martin gazed at the plate in awe. "I say, Violet, this is quite a feast."

"It is, indeed," Elizabeth agreed. "I was just saying the same thing."

Violet brought a third plate to the table and dropped onto her chair. "If you both spent less time talking and more time eating, we could all enjoy the meal."

Martin looked offended. "My, we're just the teensy bit liverish this morning, aren't we?"

Violet sent him a look that would have stopped a German tank in its tracks.

Martin wisely picked up his utensils and attacked his breakfast.

Elizabeth waited until everyone had cleared their plates and Violet had served tea before asking gently, "Violet, is something bothering you? Is there anything I can do to help?"

Violet mumbled something she didn't catch.

Elizabeth sighed and tried again. "Violet? I can't help if I don't know what it is you're worrying about."

After a moment of frowning silence, Violet put her cup back in its saucer. "It's that Mr. Forrester chap. He rang again this morning. He's staying at the Tudor Arms tonight and he wants to come over here on Monday to talk to you about that tour of the Manor House. Polly answered the telephone."

"Oh, goodness." Elizabeth's own cup clattered in its saucer. "What did she tell him?"

"She told him she'd ring him back and let him know if it was convenient. Then she told me, and now I'm telling you."

"Well, we could certainly use the money."

Violet picked up her teaspoon and sloshed it around in her tea, even though she'd already stirred it at least once. "I know, Lizzie, I know. It's just that it's going to make things awkward, what with the Americans here now."

"They're awkward, all right," Martin said, nodding his

head so hard, his glasses slipped down his nose. "Those devils can't even speak English."

"I'm not talking about the American officers," Violet said irritably. "At least they keep themselves to themselves. Which is more than I can say about some people around here."

"Well, we shall just have to manage." Elizabeth laid her serviette on the table. "As I said, we need the money. We still haven't had the water pipes seen to in the east wing, and the chimneys have to be cleaned in the next week or two. Not to mention the broken tiles on the roof, or the crack in the window in the great hall—"

"You don't have to remind me." Violet's scrawny shoulders lifted in a shrug. "If that miserable sod of a husband of yours hadn't gambled away every penny you had, we wouldn't be in this fix."

"Ex-husband," Elizabeth said carefully. "And there's no point in bringing that up. Blaming Harry for our troubles and carrying on about it is not going to solve anything. We have to put all that behind us and concentrate on what's ahead."

"You're right." Violet rubbed her forehead with bony fingers. "I'm sorry, Lizzie, I'm just out of sorts today. George and Gracie have been such a bother, and it's just one thing after another."

Elizabeth leaned back in her chair. "Oh, dear, what have they done now?"

Martin frowned. "George and Gracie? Are they guests? Not more infernal American airmen, I hope." His sparse white eyebrows lifted. "Good Lord, madam! You didn't hire more staff? I hope they know not to interfere with my duties."

"They chewed a leg of the dining room table and peed in the library," Violet said, wrinkling her nose in disgust.

Martin looked astounded. "I say, that's a bit much, isn't it?"

Elizabeth felt a stab of guilt. Ever since Major Earl

Monroe had given her the boisterous puppies, there had been one disaster after another, according to Violet. Elizabeth had promised her she'd take care of the frisky animals, but her duties as lady of the manor kept her busy most of the day, and by the time evening had come, the puppies had worn themselves out and were peacefully sleeping.

"Why don't you ask Polly to keep an eye on them?" she suggested.

Violet sniffed. "Ask Polly? All that girl can think about is Yanks. Ever since those officers from the American air base have been billeted in this house, Polly has gone around with stars in her eyes and her head stuffed full of daydreams. She spends more time in your office playing secretary than she does cleaning the house. Might as well ask Martin to take care of the little blighters."

Martin looked confused. "Take care of whom? I have enough to do in the house without having to worry about extra staff to train. Especially if they are predisposed to using the library as a lavatory. Disgusting, that's what I call it. Wouldn't be tolerated in my day."

Elizabeth patted Martin's hand. Her butler had long ago ceased to be of any real help in the mansion. His advanced age had left him somewhat senile and often confused, but both Violet and Elizabeth went to great pains to convince the old gentleman he was still an essential member of the staff. "We're talking about the new puppies, Martin. George and Gracie, remember? The ones Major Monroe was kind enough to give to me."

Martin shook his head. "Germans, bombs, Americans, dogs in the house . . . what is this world coming to, that's what I want to know. The master will be most displeased about this. Most displeased. I hate to think what he will say."

"The master's dead, Martin." Violet pushed herself

away from the table and picked up her cup and saucer. "He and Lady Hartleigh died in a London air raid, remember? God rest their souls." She glanced at Elizabeth. "Sorry, Lizzie."

Elizabeth smiled. "It's quite all right, Violet."

"You are mistaken, Violet. I see him walking the great hall every morning." Martin dabbed at his mouth with his serviette.

Violet's birdlike eyes rolled up toward the ceiling. "There he goes with the blooming ghosts again."

Martin folded his serviette into a neat square. "One simply has to wonder what will come next."

Violet wagged a finger at him. "I can tell you what's next. A cricket match, that's what. Between the Americans and the English soldiers. Now, if that doesn't give us all something to worry about, I don't know what will."

Elizabeth finished the last drop of her tea and put down her cup. "I really don't know why you are so upset about it. The town councillors thought it was a splendid idea. You know how much trouble there's been between the British army and the Americans . . . not to mention a few of the villagers as well. We thought this was a way of smoothing things out between them. You know . . . friendly rivalry and all that."

Violet jammed her fists into her bony hips. "Smoothing things out."

Elizabeth beamed and nodded.

"The way you smoothed things out at the dance in the town hall? If I remember, Ted Wilkins lost at least two dozen beer tankards he'd brought from the Tudor Arms, Rita Crumm lost the heels of her best sandals, and Bessie Bartholomew got a big dent in the bun warmer from the bakeshop in that fight."

Elizabeth's smiled faded. "Well, I admit what happened was unfortunate, but there was a lot of pent-up frustration. After all, the men of the United States Army

Air Force are risking their lives every day for us, and yet they are treated like lepers by some of the villagers, and especially by the British soldiers. If we can engage them in some friendly physical challenges, I'm hoping they can work off some of that resentment."

Violet tossed her head. "Spare me the speeches, Lizzie. I've heard it all before. All I'm saying is that getting the Limeys and the Yanks together is like putting a bunch of cats in a room full of rats. Someone is going to get hurt, and I don't want it to be you."

"I thought you said they were dogs," Martin said, shaking his head in bewilderment.

"You worry too much. Everything will work out beautifully, you'll see." Elizabeth put every ounce of confidence she could muster into her voice, but she couldn't ignore her pang of uneasiness. Violet's concerns had some grain of validity. She would simply have to exert more control over the proceedings, that was all.

"Have you had a chance to visit Henrietta Jones yet?" Violet lowered a pile of dishes into a sink full of soapy water and began rattling them around.

Grateful for the change of subject, Elizabeth said quickly, "Not yet. I haven't had time. But it's almost time I collected the rent, so I'll pop down there first thing Monday morning. Since she's a new tenant, I thought I'd take along a basket of provisions, though now that we have rationing, that might be more difficult than it was in the old days."

"I might be able to find a few things we can spare." Violet wiped her hands on her apron and headed for the larder. "Poor old soul, I feel sorry for her. Deaf as a doorpost, she is. Can't hear a word anyone says to her. Must be hard living alone in all that silence."

"That could be a blessing for some," Martin said dryly.

Elizabeth paid him scant attention. She was too busy wondering how Violet could so readily offer food from her larder for a complete stranger, when up until now she had jealously guarded the tightly rationed supplies with all the fervor of a tiger protecting its young.

Since it was Saturday night, the racket inside the public bar of the Tudor Arms had risen to an ear-splitting level. A noisy argument had broken out between the players at the dartboard, and a group of American airmen stood around a tinny-sounding piano bellowing their own bawdy version of a popular song while the enthusiastic pianist did his best to pound the keys right through to the floor.

Peering through the thick haze of cigarette smoke, Polly watched her sister carry two glasses over to the burn-pitted table. She usually looked forward to her gin and orange, especially since she wasn't supposed to be drinking. She wasn't even supposed to be in the pub. Ma would kill her if she found out. Probably kill Marlene, too. Her sister was supposed to be keeping an eye on her.

Polly took the glass from Marlene's hand and drank a large gulp of the orange liquid. The gin burned on the way down. Normally that felt good. Tonight nothing felt good.

"I hope you're not going to sit around here moping all night," Marlene said, plopping herself down on her chair. "That would be a bloody waste of good gin."

Polly shrugged. "Don't worry. I'm not going to let a bighead like Sam Cutter spoil my evening. Who needs him, anyway?"

Marlene squinted at her sister. "You do. You've been seeing him every chance you can for weeks. I thought he was the love of your life."

Polly swallowed hard. "So did I."

Marlene took a sip of her gin. "Well, if you ask me, it's just as well. You know what them Yanks are like.

You can't trust 'em for one flipping minute. Besides, Sam's too old for you."

Polly blinked back a tear. "He's not neither."

"He's at least twenty-three."

"Twenty-four."

"You're only fifteen."

"He doesn't know that. He thinks I'm twenty."

"Which makes it all the worse. What was the fight about, anyway?"

"None of your business."

Marlene shrugged. "Okay, but all I can say is good riddance to bad rubbish."

Polly opened her mouth to hurl back a retort, but at that moment a skinny Yank with scars on his face leaned across the table almost nose to nose with her.

"Hi, beautiful." He bared uneven teeth in an unpleasant grin. "Where've you been all my life?"

Polly pulled back, out of range of his beery breath. "Dodging creeps like you."

"Aw, come on, you don't mean that." The Yank perched a hip on the table. "Tell you what, sugar. How about showing me the sights of this little town? We could take a beer on the beach—"

"You can take a bloody jump off the cliff," Marlene butted in. "She told you, she's not interested."

The airman's slitted gaze slid over Marlene. "Who asked you, bigmouth?"

Something about the look in the Yank's eyes made Polly's skin crawl. "Here," she said, doing her best to put some authority in her voice, "why don't you just sod off and leave us alone."

The airman leaned over her again. "What's the matter, sugar, not good enough for you, is that it? Well, maybe I should show you just how good I can be."

He put his hand on Polly's shoulder and she shook it off. "Bugger off, or I'll tell Alfie. He'll throw you out on your bloody ear."

"Aw, honey, you know he's not gonna do that—"

The Yank's words ended in a gasp as a large hand from behind him closed over his mouth. "Maybe not, but I sure will," said a gruff voice.

Polly felt a rush of excitement at the sight of the tall American standing behind her tormentor. "Sam!"

Sam ignored her, his grim gaze fixed on the man in his grasp. "Get lost, Kenny. Go find someone else to bug."

Kenny's chin lifted. "Who's gonna make me?"

"I am." Sam pushed his face into Kenny's. "So make it easy on yourself, okay?"

Afraid there might be trouble, Polly said quickly, "It's all right, Sam. He wasn't doing no harm. He was just leaving."

"See?" Kenny bared his teeth in another grin. "She liked it. You're outta luck, soldier. Find yourself another girl. This one's mine."

Polly straightened her back. "Here, I never said that."

Sam grabbed Kenny by the collar. "You lay one hand on her, Morris, and you're dead."

"Tell him, sugar," Kenny sneered. "Tell him how you've been begging me to put my hands on you."

Polly gasped, then gasped again when Sam brought back his fist and smashed it into Kenny's leering face. With a howl Kenny leaped forward and the two men went down, throwing wild punches at each other.

The Yanks at the piano stopped singing and surged torward them. Polly jumped to her feet, but lost sight of Sam as the men crowded around the two wrestling on the floor.

Marlene grabbed her hand and gave it a sharp tug. "Come on, Polly, we'd better get out of here. If Ma hears about this, she'll kill us both."

"Wait, I want to talk to Sam. I've got to see if he's all right." Polly struggled to see what was going on inside the circle of shouting and gesturing men.

"Come *on*," Marlene yelled, and dragged her unwilling sister toward the door. "We'll catch hell from Ma if we don't get out of here now."

There wasn't much Polly could do but go along with her. Marlene was right, she'd be up to her neck in trouble if Ma found out they were down there and started a fight. In any case, she couldn't very well speak to Sam while he was scrapping. All she could hope was that he wouldn't get hurt.

A warm feeling crept over her as she scurried along the street in an effort to keep up with Marlene. Her Sam had fought for her. That was the best thing anyone had ever done for her. That was something she'd never forget her whole blooming life.

Sundays in Sitting Marsh were usually quite peaceful. People got up late, went to church, tended their gardens in the summer, and hibernated indoors in the winter. Occasionally a fete or a garden show would break up the monotony, but for the most part, Sundays in the village were pretty much guaranteed to be uneventful.

This Sunday was no exception. Elizabeth spent the day catching up on her correspondence—blissfully without the distraction of Polly's chatter. Sundays were her part-secretary, part-housemaid's day off, and Elizabeth made the most of it.

Early that evening she exercised George and Gracie, exerting more energy than both puppies combined chasing them away from the piles of raked leaves, and out of the flower beds and ornamental shrubs. Desmond, her gardener, had already expressed his outrage at having to clean up after the dogs. Damage to the gardens would certainly add fuel to his fire.

Now that the nights were drawing in, she had less time to spend outdoors. The chill in the air was becoming more pronounced, and if she didn't organize the cricket match soon, it would be too cold to play.

She fell asleep that night thinking about the match, and was woken up out of a dream where she was umpiring a game played entirely by dogs. At first she couldn't think what had awakened her, until she heard the distinct sound of bells. She recognized them instantly. The church bells in the spire of St. Matthew's.

Sleepily she reached for her bedside lamp and switched it on. The hands on her alarm clock pointed to five past three. While she was still struggling to make sense of why church bells would ring in the middle of the night, a heavy pounding startled her into full consciousness.

"Lizzie!" Violet's voice called out urgently. "Lizzie, get up! It's the bells."

Elizabeth stumbled out of bed, grabbed her dressing gown from the back of a chair, and tugged it on as she crossed the thick carpet to the door. She had never locked her bedroom door until a contingent of American airmen had been billeted at the Manor House by the war office. Although she was quite sure that the American officers were all perfect gentlemen, the sense of security the locked door gave her allowed her to sleep more peacefully.

Violet's thin face was chalk white when Elizabeth threw open the door. Her frizzy gray hair stood out straight from her head. Obviously she hadn't had a chance to brush it.

Alarmed by the sense of urgency, Elizabeth demanded sharply, "What is it? Is it an air raid? What's happened?"

Violet clutched the neck of her pink candlewick dressing gown. "It's the signal, Lizzie. Don't you remember? The signal for an invasion. It's the Germans. They've come for us. They're invading the village."

CHAPTER

❀ 2 ❀

Martin had insisted on getting fully dressed in his usual
dark suit and waistcoat, and by the time Elizabeth had
convinced him he was safe at the house with Violet for
the time being, it seemed quite likely the entire village
would be overrun with gun-waving German soldiers.

She was immensely relieved, therefore, upon reaching
St. Matthew's, to discover that the disoriented crowd
milling around the churchyard consisted of mostly villagers and a handful of Americans huddled together next
to their jeeps.

The bells had ceased their mournful summons, and
the full moon cast an eerie glow over the scene, throwing the tall spire of St. Matthew's into a dark silhouette
against the clear night sky.

Elizabeth spied Rita Crumm, dressed in baggy slacks
and a thick sweater, bellowing orders to a shivering
group of housewives. Every one of them held some kind

of garden implement in her hand. Rakes and shovels seemed the most popular, though Florrie Evans, the most insipid of Rita's homegrown army, clung to a frying pan with all the determination of potted shrimp.

Rita, who fancied herself as a sort of self-made general, was apparently doing her best to organize her reluctant troops into a feasible barrier against the advancing enemy. Rita was under the mistaken impression that given enough determination, she could tackle the entire German army single-handedly. She made no secret of her inherent belief that her war efforts would exemplify every glorified heroine in history.

Right now all she appeared to be achieving was a sore throat from yelling at her confused entourage.

The few men left in the village, those too old, too unhealthy, or too valuable for civilian life to join the military, were assembled at the far edge of the crowd and seemed to be earnestly discussing the proper procedure for withstanding an invasion.

As yet there were no signs of the only real official form of authority—the constabulary, which wasn't all that surprising considering the entire police force of Sitting Marsh consisted of two elderly and somewhat dense constables dragged out of retirement after the army had snagged the vast majority of England's able-bodied men.

Not too far from where Elizabeth parked her motorcycle—her sole means of transportation—Polly and her sister, Marlene, stood arguing with their mother, who was no doubt insisting that the girls return to the security of their home.

No one seemed to know what was going on, and deciding that someone needed to take charge, Elizabeth went in search of Major Earl Monroe. As lady of the manor, she was duty bound to supervise proceedings until the police arrived. She wasn't quite sure why she felt that the commanding officer of her enforced houseguests would be the most help under the circumstances, but it was an awfully good excuse to seek him out. She hadn't seen the major alone in almost a week, and she missed his enjoyable company.

It wasn't until she caught sight of him climbing down from a jeep—in the same moment he saw her—that she realized she probably wasn't looking her best. She hadn't had time to do much with her hair, which, instead of being neatly arranged on her head in its accustomed French roll, was tucked rather haphazardly into a hairnet.

Her face was completely naked of powder and lipstick, she had been unable to find clean stockings that weren't laddered, and the pleated black skirt she wore under her gray wool coat needed ironing. Her mother, the late Lady Hartleigh and pinnacle of good taste, would turn in her grave.

It was too late to worry about her appearance now, however, since Major Monroe was already striding toward her. He greeted her with his usual casual salute. "Glad you're here, Lady Elizabeth. People are sure getting jittery."

A tremendous feeling of well-being washed over her as she answered his greeting. Somehow Earl Monroe always made her feel on top of the world, no matter what disaster was rocking it at that moment. In fact, such was the effect he had on her, she was constantly reminding herself that the major had a wife and family back in the States, and could be of no possible importance in her life. Not that it seemed to help much.

"Does anyone know what's going on?" She gestured at the crowd. "Apparently everyone's talking about an invasion. If the Germans are indeed invading us, they obviously haven't reached the village yet."

Earl peered up the road in the direction of the beach as if he expected a battalion of tanks to come rolling around the bend. "That's what I heard. That's why we're here. I sent a couple of guys to check out the coast road. They should be back any minute."

Elizabeth glanced at the church. "Does anyone know who rang the bells? Have you seen the vicar?"

"I saw him a minute ago talking to that woman with the loud voice." Earl nodded in Rita's direction. "She's some lady. I could hear her a mile down the road."

Elizabeth sighed. "Take no notice of Rita. . . . she's quite harmless, actually."

She winced as Rita screeched yet another order. The housewives shuffled into an uneven line, standing shoulder to shoulder.

Earl grinned. "Rakes and brooms against bayonets. You gotta admire their guts."

"Or pity their stupidity," Elizabeth said briskly. "I—" She broke off as the roar of an engine echoed from farther down the road.

The sound effectively silenced everyone, even Rita, as they all turned to face the coast road. For a moment Elizabeth felt sick with fright, until she realized that the German army would hardly advance with a single vehicle. The travelers had to be Earl's men.

Nevertheless, she held her breath as she watched the jeep approach. From somewhere behind her she heard a quavery voice wail, "Oo, 'eck," and Rita's sharp voice answering, "Hush! Stand your ground, ladies."

"You stand it," someone muttered. "I'm going back to my kids."

A chorus of "Me, too" followed the statement, and a clatter suggested the weapons had been cast to the ground as the women scurried out of the line of fire.

Rita's howl of protest died as the jeep pulled to a halt in front of Earl and two American officers jumped out.

Elizabeth recognized one of them as Sam Cutter, the young man who was responsible for Polly's constant state of bemusement these days. He lifted his hand in a sloppy salute. "Nothing going on down there, sir. False alarm, I reckon." As he turned his head, Elizabeth noticed a dark bruise just under his left eye. Or maybe it was a shadow. In that light she couldn't be sure.

"That's what I figured," Earl said. "Thanks, Sam."

Elizabeth relaxed her shoulders. "That's a relief." She turned and waved at the silent crowd. "All right, everyone, back to your beds. There's no invasion tonight."

"Are you quite sure, your ladyship?" Rita demanded.

She actually sounded disappointed, Elizabeth thought sourly. "Quite sure, Rita. The invasion would have come from the beach, and there's only one road into town. If the Germans have launched an invasion, they are not advancing on Sitting Marsh."

"Which wouldn't make a whole lot of sense anyway, if you think about it," Earl murmured.

Elizabeth raised her hand as a babble of voices arose from the crowd. "I would like to know which one of you raised the alarm, however. I'm sure it was well-intentioned, so don't be embarrassed to admit it. It would help put our minds at ease to know who it was, and why."

Silence greeted her question as everyone looked blankly at one another.

"I was one of the first to get here, m'm." Percy Bodkins, the grocer, raised his hand. "I didn't see no one come out of the church."

"That's right, your ladyship. He was here when I got here." Bessie Bartholomew, the plump and jovial owner of the bake shop and tea room, pumped her head up and down. " 'T were only Percy, Rita, Clara and her lads, and the vicar when I got here."

A white-haired man in a shabby raincoat pushed his way forward. The collar at his throat gleamed white in the moonlight, and reflected on the thick lenses of his glasses. "Lady Elizabeth, I don't know who rang the bells, but whoever it was must have run off afterward. Just a prank, I'm thinking."

"You're probably right, Reverend." Elizabeth nodded at the vicar. "Perhaps we should take a quick look in the bell tower, however. I would hate to think that someone would do any damage to the church, but I would feel better if we inspected the tower, just in case."

"Well, I don't know how much we can see in the dark," the Reverend Roland Cumberland said doubtfully. "Perhaps we should wait until morning. There are no lights in there—"

"Here," Sam said, reaching into the jeep. "I've got a flashlight."

The vicar looked confused. "Flashlight?"

"He means a torch," a young voice said helpfully.

Elizabeth watched Polly step forward and stand close to Sam. She gazed up at him with adoration shining in her face. Sam looked as if he didn't quite know what to say, but then was spared of saying anything when a thin woman stepped up and pulled on Polly's arm. "Come on, my girl, it's high time you went home to bed."

"Aw, Ma!" Polly kept her gaze on Sam. "See you tomorrow?"

The young man seemed embarrassed but gave her a quick nod.

Polly blew him a kiss, then, still grumbling, allowed her mother to lead her off down the road, with Marlene dragging behind them.

Earl switched on the flashlight and pointed it at the church. "Okay, let's take a look." He waved a hand at the small group of Americans. "You guys get back to the house. There's nothing more you can do here."

He waited until the officers had pulled away in the jeep before leading the way into the churchyard. "Is the tower locked?" he asked as he paused in front of the heavy wooden door.

The vicar shook his head. "There's no need. There isn't anything in there to steal, unless someone wants to cart away the bells."

"They'd have to get them down first," Elizabeth remarked. She stood behind Earl Monroe's broad back, enjoying the feeling of security his presence gave her.

Earl stretched out a hand and pushed on the door. It groaned in protest, then swung open with a loud creak.

Elizabeth peered over Earl's shoulder as the beam of his flashlight swept over the floor, then the walls. Something scuttled away in the darkness, and at the same moment, a loud screech and a flapping of wings from the tower above sent a shiver down Elizabeth's back.

"Owl, your ladyship," the vicar remarked in her ear, making her jump.

Earl stepped into the tower, then made his way across the damp floorboards that squeaked with every step. Elizabeth followed, though much more slowly, while the reverend brought up the rear.

The door of the inner tower creaked open and Earl stepped through, the wide, bright shaft of light sweeping the floor in front of him. Then he stopped short, so suddenly, Elizabeth bumped into him, and the strangled sound he uttered made her blood run cold.

"What is it?"

Her fierce whisper sounded loud as it bounced off the walls, but Earl seemed not to hear. He was staring at the corner of the room, where the beam of light trembled on a dark shape hanging from the bell rope.

The vicar muttered something under his breath and started praying.

At first, Elizabeth thought it was a sack of corn. She looked closer, then bit her tongue as her teeth clamped down on a scream. It wasn't a sack at all. It was a young man, and judging from his blank, staring eyes, and the way his tongue protruded horribly from his mouth, he was beyond any help they could give him.

Earl insisted on driving Elizabeth home, promising to take her back the next morning to retrieve her motorcycle. He waited until the door opened, embarrassing Elizabeth no end when Martin appeared waving the ancient rusted blunderbuss that had been the centerpiece of her father's gun collection.

Violet, who had apparently heard the jeep arrive, was also at the door, trying in vain to convince the befuddled butler that they were not being attacked by the Germans. In all the confusion, Earl quietly left, without giving Elizabeth the opportunity to say a proper good night to him.

The Americans had their own entrance into the east wing where they were quartered, though Elizabeth often suggested that Earl use the main entrance rather than walk around the vast building to the east door. This was one night in particular when she would have preferred his company for a while longer.

Still shaken, she accepted Violet's offer of hot cocoa, then sat in the kitchen to drink it while she recounted the night's events. Fortunately Martin, once he had been assured that there were no signs of an invasion, had chosen to return to his bed.

Violet, of course, was horrified that Elizabeth had been exposed to such a terrible experience. "Do you know who he was?" She stared at Elizabeth with eyes as big as saucers. "Who would do such a thing?"

Elizabeth sighed. "The young man was an American officer. His name was Kenny Morris. Earl recognized him, though I don't know how." She shuddered. "His face was horribly distorted."

"Ugh!" Violet wrapped her fingers around her mug. "An American? Oh, blimey, that'll cause problems for us. I'm willing to bet on that."

"I'm afraid you might be right. Knowing how many of the villagers feel about the Americans, it does rather make things look bad for them."

"Maybe he hung himself."

"I don't think so. His feet were on the ground with his knees buckled."

"You don't think one of our blokes did it, do you?"

"I don't know." Elizabeth looked miserably at her housekeeper. "There is so much fighting going on at the Tudor Arms, I suppose it was only a matter of time before someone got really hurt."

Violet shook her head. "Doesn't make sense. I always thought it was just a bunch of chaps blowing off steam. I never dreamed it would come to murdering each other. What did George and Sid say?"

"Not much. They didn't arrive until we were leaving the church."

"Not much good as policemen, are they? Those two are always the last to know when something bad happens."

Inwardly Elizabeth agreed. Nevertheless, she felt compelled to defend the inept village constables. "Sid didn't hear the bells. He's hard of hearing and as you know, he lives alone. It took George some time to wake him up. By the time they rode their bicycles into the village, almost everyone had gone home."

"As usual." Violet made a sound of disgust. "So no one knows what happened."

"All we know is that Kenny Morris was apparently strangled with a bell rope. We don't know when, why, or by whom. I imagine the constables will sort things out."

Violet grunted. "Don't count on it. What about the Americans? If it's one of theirs, won't they want to investigate the murder?"

"I suppose they will. Earl will be giving them a report in the morning and make arrangements to collect the body. I feel so awful about the poor parents. Imagine worrying about your son being shot down in an airplane, and then finding out he'd been murdered. What a terrible tragedy." She drained the last of her cocoa. "I'm really tired, Violet. I must go back to bed. I have to meet with Mr. Forrester in a few hours and I need to make a good impression."

"Seems to me he's the one who needs to make a good impression." Violet tipped her head to one side. "You can always make an excuse not to show the house, you know. After all, now that we have Americans billeted here, that makes a difference."

Elizabeth gave her a tired smile. "I'd like to do that, Violet, but we really do need the money."

"I suppose you're right." Violet patted her on the shoulder. "Go to bed, Lizzie. I'll see you in the morning."

Elizabeth needed no second bidding. The moment her head touched the pillow, she was sound asleep, and she didn't wake up until long after the sun had cleared the tops of the elm trees lining the driveway.

"I don't think I'll have time to take the dogs out this morning," she told Violet, as she sat rather wearily at the kitchen table later. "Mr. Forrester will be arriving in less than an hour."

She noticed with concern the dark shadows under Violet's eyes when the housekeeper turned from the stove. "Don't worry." Violet stifled a yawn. "Polly took them out when she got here."

Elizabeth's eyebrows raised. "Polly? She usually buries herself in the office as soon as she gets here. Ever since I told her she could assist me in there, she's practically taken over. I must admit, I didn't think she would be all that much help."

"Don't I know it." Violet carried a plate of sausage, eggs, fried tomatoes, and crisp fried bread to the table. "She's getting a little too big for her boots, if you ask me. She told me the other day she doesn't have time to clean the bathrooms properly, now that she's got all the office work to do."

"Oh, dear." Elizabeth bit into a piece of toast. "Perhaps we should think about hiring another housemaid."

"Good luck with that. No one wants to clean houses

anymore. They're all working in the factories or on the land."

"Surely there must still be some people willing to do housework."

"The only way you'll get someone is to give them room and board, like you do me and Martin. That way you could get someone down from London. There must be a lot of women anxious to get out of there with all the bombing going on."

"I suppose you're right." Elizabeth sighed. "I'll look into it, though I'm not sure we can afford it."

"Maybe Polly will take less money if she doesn't have to do the housework."

"I suppose it wouldn't hurt to ask her."

"Well, you'd better wait for a day or two. She's really upset about that murder last night."

"I'm not surprised." Elizabeth picked up her knife and fork. "Murder is upsetting to everyone."

"Especially when you know the poor devil."

Elizabeth stared at her housekeeper. "Polly knew Kenny Morris?"

"So did that American officer she's always hanging around with . . . Sam, I think it is."

"Sam Cutter? How do you know about this?"

"Polly told me, didn't she." Violet sat down at the table. "What's more, she told me that Sam and this Kenny person had a big fight in the Tudor Arms on Saturday night. She wouldn't say what over, but I got the idea she was mixed up in it somehow."

Elizabeth slowly put down her knife and fork. "Sam was fighting with Kenny Morris?"

Violet nodded, her face clouded with worry. "You don't think Polly will be in trouble, do you?"

"I hope not." Elizabeth rose from her chair. "But I think I'd better have a word with her straight away." She didn't voice her fears aloud, but she knew by Violet's expression that her housekeeper shared her concern. Maybe it was a coincidence that Kenny Morris died the night after having a fight with Sam Cutter. And maybe not.

CHAPTER

3

Elizabeth heard the shrill ring of the telephone before she reached the door of her study. Polly must have picked it up almost immediately, since she didn't hear it ring again. By the time she'd opened the door, Polly had replaced the receiver in its cradle.

"Oh, there you are, m'm," she exclaimed, as Elizabeth entered the cluttered room. "I was just telling the major—"

Elizabeth cut her off with a sharp exclamation. "That was Major Monroe? Did he say what he wanted?"

Polly shook her dark head. "No, m'm. Just that he wanted to speak to you. I offered to come and get you, but he said he had to go, but he'd ring back later."

Disappointed at having missed a chance to talk to Earl, Elizabeth picked up the stack of invoices from the tray. "Thank you, Polly. I suppose we should sort these out and see which ones we can pay this month."

"Yes, m'm."

Polly sounded subdued, and not at all her usual ebullient self. Elizabeth sat down on the roomy armchair by the window and tried not to sound too concerned when she said, "Violet tells me you knew the young man we found murdered in the church tower last night."

Polly jumped as if she'd been stung. "I didn't know him really. Just sort of met him once. Well . . . I didn't meet him, neither. He just spoke to me, that's all."

Elizabeth studied her secretary's red face. "It's all right, Polly. I'm not accusing you of doing anything wrong. I was just wondering if you heard anything that could help us find out what happened to him."

Polly shook her head so violently, a couple of hairpins fell from her dark hair to the desk. "I don't know nothing, m'm. Honest I don't."

"Violet says that nice young American Sam Cutter knew him as well."

Polly's flush deepened. "Well, I s'pose he would, seeing as how they are in the same unit."

"I think it's a little more than that, isn't it, Polly?" Elizabeth asked gently.

Polly nodded miserably.

"Would you like to tell me about it?"

Elizabeth listened carefully as Polly described the scene down at the Tudor Arms.

"So you didn't see Sam after the fight, then?"

"No, m'm, I didn't. But I know my Sam would never do nothing like killing someone. I just know he wouldn't, that's all."

Elizabeth leaned back in the chair and sighed. "I hope you're right, Polly. I'd hate to think that you were involved with someone who could get you into a lot of trouble."

Polly straightened her shoulders as if she were ready to take on the world. "Yes, m'm."

Sensing that the young girl had nothing useful to add,

Elizabeth changed the subject. "Well, let's get on with the work, then. I'd like to get these taken care of before Mr. Forrester arrives."

She sorted through the invoices, wondering what was so important that Earl Monroe couldn't have waited until he got back to the Manor House that evening to tell her.

She didn't have too much time to worry about Earl, since Brian Forrester arrived shortly before eleven, taking her away from the task of making arrangements to tour the cricket pavilion. Since the pavilion had been out of use for so long, she was concerned about the state of the establishment. If they were going to have a cricket match in the next week or two, no doubt there would be some pretty drastic cleaning to be done.

When Martin announced the arrival of her visitor, she was somewhat irritated at being disturbed.

It didn't help when Martin muttered out of the side of his mouth as he opened the door of the library, "Bit of a pompous ass, madam, if you ask me."

"No one did, Martin," she reminded him. "Ask Violet to send up some coffee and biscuits, please."

"Yes, madam." Martin's expression suggested that Violet's coffee was far superior for the likes of Brian Forrester, but he had the good grace not to voice his opinion.

Elizabeth fixed a smile on her face and swept into the room, while Martin announced in his quavery voice, "Lady Elizabeth Hartleigh Compton. Mr. Forrester, your ladyship."

A thick-set man rose from his chair and turned to face her. She couldn't help noticing the raw redness of his cheeks and nose, suggesting that the man had a strong attachment to alcohol. His sandy hair was sprinkled liberally with gray, and his light blue eyes seemed to disappear beneath heavy, drooping lids.

His pale gaze was quite insolent as it lingered over

her from head to toe, leaving her with the unpleasant feeling of having been violated in some way. "It's a great pleasure to meet you, your ladyship," he said, giving her an old-fashioned bow that seemed only to ridicule her.

"Mr. Forrester. Nice of you to come."

"Nice of you to invite me, your ladyship. Very nice home you have here. Very nice. I especially like the dark paneling." He threw out his hand in an expansive gesture. "Very effect—" He broke off with a wince and rubbed his shoulder.

Elizabeth felt compelled to ask, "Something wrong?"

Forrester shook his head. "Slight sprain, that's all. I was moving some furniture for one of the old-agers. Old age creeping up on me as well, I suppose."

His loud laugh irritated her, and she said quickly, "I understand you want to escort a tour of my home."

"That's right, Lady Elizabeth. That *is* the right title, is it not?"

Elizabeth inclined her head in graceful acknowledgment. "So, when can we expect you, and how many?"

Forrester rubbed his pudgy hands together. "Ah, well, I have a busload of elderly people just dying to see your beautiful home, your ladyship. Just dying. You'll like our old-agers. Terrific group of people they are. So grateful for everything I do for them. Makes it a pleasure to take them out. That it does, indeed."

The unexpected revelation surprised her. "You take them out often?"

"As often as I can. I like to get them out of London now and then. For most of them I'm the only person outside their homes who cares whether they live or die. Sad, isn't it?"

Elizabeth had to agree. "Very sad. I'm glad that we can provide a respite for them."

"Of course, if they could all meet you personally, that

would really mean a lot to them, your ladyship. I'm sure they won't be any trouble."

"Regretfully, Mr. Forrester, my duties prevent me from socializing with the sightseers. My private quarters will be off limits, I'm afraid, and I should warn you that the war office has billeted several American officers with us, which will mean the east wing is also out of bounds."

Forrester's bushy eyebrows raised. "Americans? In the Manor House? Surely you can't be serious?"

"Perfectly serious, Mr. Forrester. One has to make sacrifices nowadays. Providing accommodations for some of the heroes who are fighting our war in the skies is a small thing to ask, under the circumstances."

"I'd say that having to put up with those loud-mouthed, insolent troublemakers is asking far too much from a lady such as yourself. What in damnation is the war office thinking? Don't they have any respect for the aristocracy these days?"

Elizabeth lifted her chin. "I can assure you, Mr. Forrester, the Americans are perfect gentlemen, and will have no adverse effect on your tour, apart from eliminating the east wing, that is." She longed to tell this obnoxious man that it was none of his business whom she entertained in her home, but good manners compelled her to refrain.

Instead, she informed him, "A vast section of the Manor House will be open to you, however, and the gardens are quite beautiful, even at this time of year. Since your clients are elderly, I think they will find the experience strenuous enough as it is."

"Well, I suppose you're right." Forrester glanced at his watch. "I don't like to push them too hard, you know. They enjoy these outings so much, they tend to overdo things sometimes. I just hope we don't run into any of the American chaps, though. Might get the old dears a little too excited."

"I'm quite sure the American officers will be far too

busy trying to stay alive in the skies to interrupt your tour," Elizabeth said dryly. "Now, if you will just give me the date you wish to come, I'll have my secretary write out an invoice for you. Payment is due by the day of the tour."

"Not to worry." Forrester pulled a checkbook from his jacket pocket with a flourish. "We'll be down next Saturday, if that's all right with you. Just tell me the amount and you'll have your money today."

Elizabeth could feel her cheeks burning as she returned to the office. Martin was right in his estimation. Brian Forrester was a pompous ass. How she hated being beholden to a man like that. Still, he seemed to genuinely care about his elderly charges, and as she had told Violet several times already, they really did need the money.

She sent Polly back with the invoice and an apology, saying her duties prevented her from returning that day. A few minutes later she heard the growl of a motorcar engine. Glancing out of the window, she saw, with relief, a black sedan retreating a little too fast down the driveway. At least she wouldn't have to deal with the man again.

Violet would be conducting the tour, with the help of Polly, and no doubt Martin, who would be prowling in the background keeping an alert eye on everything. Martin might not be able to move too swiftly, but he could sound quite imperative when provoked.

Thus satisfied that she had fulfilled her obligation to the cause, she spent the rest of the day wondering what it was that Earl Monroe was so anxious to tell her.

Elizabeth had to wait until after dinner that evening before she had a chance to talk to Earl. She was seated on her white wicker divan in the conservatory, when Violet announced that the major wished to see her.

Elizabeth was rather pleased with her timing. She had

been hoping that Earl might visit her while she was enjoying an after-dinner sherry in her favorite sanctuary. The glass walls overlooked the vast lawns of the Manor House grounds, affording a magnificent view of the gardens in daylight. Desmond had stocked the room with tropical plants, and their fragrance filled the air, evoking visions of exotic islands in far-off seas. At night, with the thick blackout curtains at the windows obliterating the view and the wind rustling the poplars, one could almost imagine palm trees swaying outside under velvet skies, with gentle waves lapping on a warm beach just a few yards away.

Spending time here was like escaping to another world, and there was no one with whom Elizabeth enjoyed the retreat more than Major Monroe. After ordering Violet to bring the remainder of the sherry and another glass, she settled back to enjoy the rest of the evening.

Earl seemed even more tense than usual when he entered the room. An energetic man, he appeared to have great difficulty in relaxing, even under normal circumstances. Elizabeth knew that he missed the wide-open plains and vast, empty skies of his home in Wyoming, and at times felt constricted by the tiny, winding lanes and neat, checkerboard fields of Sitting Marsh.

Also, the stress of his job had to be horrendous. Having to be responsible for sending young men into life-threatening situations every day was a constant source of worry for him, and Elizabeth took great pride in her ability to smooth away the frowns that marred his pleasant face.

There were times, however, when she failed to erase the agony that tormented him when an airplane failed to come home, or crash-landed full of holes on the base. And it happened far too often lately. By the look on Earl's face tonight, this was one of those times.

"Sit down," she said, after he'd greeted her with a

tired smile. "A nice glass of sherry will help chase that unflattering scowl away."

"Sorry, was I frowning?" He took the glass from her hand and waited until she was seated again before dropping into his favorite rocking chair. "I reckon that's becoming a permanent expression these days."

She searched his face, trying to read his mood.

"Bad day?"

"No more than usual. How're George and Gracie?"

"Driving Violet crazy. She has them penned in the scullery at night so they can't run all over the house. I'm afraid it's taking time to train them. They seem to think the library and the drawing room are the appropriate places to relieve themselves."

"Oh, Lord. I reckon I've given you all a mess of trouble with those dogs."

"Not at all. We adore the puppies. They've brought new life into this house. Even Martin manages to stoop down to pat them on the head when he thinks no one is looking."

Earl looked surprised. "I didn't think anything got to that old boy."

"Not much does," Elizabeth admitted. "There are times when I really worry about his senility, but somehow he always manages to rise above it." She paused, then voiced the question uppermost in her mind. "Have you heard any more about Kenny Morris?"

Earl shook his head, and sipped at his sherry before putting the fragile glass down on the marble-topped table between them. "Not much, anyway. The investigating officers did find a knife stained with blood, but they have no idea who it belongs to."

Elizabeth raised her eyebrows. "He was stabbed? I thought he was strangled with the bell rope."

"He was. The bloodstains didn't come from Morris—there wasn't a mark on him from a knife. Which means whoever killed him probably got cut in the fight. There were signs of a pretty violent struggle."

Elizabeth shuddered. "How awful. Poor man. I can't help feeling sorry for his parents, too. What a dreadful shock this must be."

"Yeah, I heard they took it pretty bad. I guess it might have been easier for them if he'd gone down in the Channel. Losing him this way is so damn senseless." He shot her a guilty glance. "Sorry, ma'am. Didn't mean to curse."

"You curse away, Major," Elizabeth said cheerfully. "As I've told you before, I've been known to mutter a swear word once or twice myself."

He leaned forward, his hands thrust between his knees. "Elizabeth, I need you to do something for me, if you will?"

She would promise him the earth as long as he went on calling her by her first name. They had agreed some time ago that he could drop her title as long as they were alone, but it was the first time since then that he'd done so. The small token of familiarity pleased her as nothing else could.

"I'll do whatever I can, of course."

"The villagers won't talk to our investigators. You know how they are."

She did indeed. The people of Sitting Marsh had made no secret of their animosity toward the Americans. Loath to trust any outsiders in their midst, the villagers viewed the Yanks with as much confidence as they would visitors from the moon.

"You want me to talk to them, is that it?"

Earl's frown deepened. "I don't want you involved in the murder in any way, but we're getting nowhere, and the villagers trust you. They'll tell you what they won't tell us. I just want you to keep your ears open and pass along anything you think might be helpful."

"Of course I will." I'll do a lot more than that, she

added inwardly. She was becoming quite experienced at solving murders, having brought two killers to justice already. Since she couldn't rely on George and Sid to unravel the mystery of poor Kenny Morris's death, she would conduct her own investigation. There was no point, however, in alarming Earl with that decision.

Instead she turned the conversation to more mundane matters. "I'm hoping to arrange the cricket match for next week. Will your men be able to get away to play?"

Earl clasped his hands across his chest. "I'm pretty sure it can be arranged. Our CO thinks it will do the men good to have a break, so he's all for it. As long as our duties don't get in the way, I don't see why we shouldn't be there."

"That's wonderful!" She leaned forward eagerly. "Will you captain the American team?"

He looked startled. "I've never played cricket."

"I would imagine that few of your men have played the game. But what about baseball? Didn't you tell me you played in high school?"

Earl shrugged. "I guess."

"Well, then, it's the same principle. The local men are willing to hold a rehearsal and teach all of you the rudiments of the game. None of them are expert, so it shouldn't be too one-sided."

He laughed, warming that special place in her heart. "I appreciate your optimism, but I have to tell you, from what I've seen, the difference between baseball and cricket is like comparing hamburgers with fish and chips. They're both food, but that's about all they have in common."

Elizabeth sighed. "I suppose it is a silly idea."

"I didn't say that. I reckon the guys would enjoy learning how to play, on one condition."

"Name it, Major."

"That we hold a return match. We'll play cricket with your guys, if they'll play baseball with ours."

She caught her breath. "What a splendid idea! Done." She held out her hand, and caught her breath when Earl folded his strong fingers around hers. To cover her confusion, she quickly withdrew her hand and said somewhat unsteadily, "I'm having the chimneys swept this week. Then we'll be able to light the fires again. Your men must be feeling the chill now that the evenings are drawing in."

"No one's complaining." His eyes wrinkled at the corners when he smiled at her. "I don't want you to go to any trouble on our behalf."

"No trouble at all. We have the chimneys cleaned every year. They get very sooty, you know."

"Does everyone heat their homes with coal fires?"

"Most everyone. Some of the bigger houses in London have heating systems, but here in the country we all have to rely on a coal fire." She glanced at him, feeling somewhat defensive. "Don't they have coal fires in America?"

"I guess so, though a lot of folks use wood-burning stoves. Most people I know have central heating."

"You have heating in your house?"

"Yes, ma'am. Oil furnace. Heats the whole house."

She sighed at the thought of such luxury. "How wonderful. I wonder if we shall ever be as modern as America. From what I've heard, England is a full century behind."

Earl laughed. "Not that bad, is it?"

"You tell me. After all, you've experienced both sides of the Atlantic."

"It's hardly a fair comparison. Things are bound to be more difficult in wartime."

"Maybe, but you have to admit, America is far ahead of us when it comes to technology in the home. Look at the motorcar, for instance. Doesn't everyone drive one over there?"

Earl shrugged. "It's a lot tougher to get around in the

States. It's more spread out. No buses or trains to take us everywhere we want to go like you have here. Sometimes you can drive for hours and not see a single house. I can't imagine doing that here."

Elizabeth gazed at him, filled with an aching, restless longing she didn't fully understand. "Oh, how I'd love to see it all."

He grinned at her. "Maybe one day you will, when the war is over."

Her despondency worried her. Normally she didn't let things get her down. One lived for the hour these days, and didn't give much thought to the next. There were times, however, when she wondered if the war would ever end. She'd almost forgotten what it was like to live without rationing and shortages in a village deprived of its able-bodied men.

One day, she supposed, things would get back to normal. Whatever normal would be by then. Certainly things would never go back to the way they were. Maybe that was a good thing. What saddened her most of all was the thought that once the war was over, Major Earl Monroe of the United States Army Air Force would return to his wife and family in America. And that thought depressed her in a way that was highly inappropriate.

CHAPTER

❈ 4 ❈

Elizabeth wasted no time the following morning. After another of Violet's surprisingly abundant breakfasts, she took the puppies for a frolic on the lawn, then loaded a basket of provisions into the sidecar of her motorcycle. After informing Violet that she was paying a visit to Henrietta Jones, she rode her motorcycle into town.

The skies were clear that morning, though the sea mist planted droplets on the wisps of hair that escaped from the warm scarf she'd wound around her head. Normally she would rejoice in the tepid warmth of the autumn sun. These days, however, a clear sky meant that a bombing mission over Europe was a certainty. Even as the thought surfaced, she heard the drone of engines overhead.

Looking up, she saw a formation of bombers flying steadily toward the ocean with their Hurricane escorts. The feeling of dread that was never very far from her mind almost numbed her. She whispered a quiet prayer before swooping down the hill toward St. Matthew's churchyard.

The gray stone walls of the ancient church towered above her in silent disapproval as she parked her motorcycle on the grass verge. Her footsteps crunched up the gravel driveway, disturbing the quiet peace of the cemetery. She'd intended to take a look in the bell tower before talking to the vicar, but to her dismay a grim-faced man in the uniform of the American military police barred her way at the door.

"Sorry, ma'am," he announced crisply. "These premises are off limits until further notice."

"Oh, that's all right, Captain." Elizabeth smiled sweetly. "Major Earl Monroe asked me to look around."

"It's corporal, ma'am, and I have orders to let no one pass."

"Well, I can see your predicament, Captain—"

"Corporal, ma'am."

"Ah, yes, Corporal." Elizabeth did her best to look regal. "Anyway, since you apparently do not recognize me, I shall introduce myself. I'm Lady Elizabeth Hartleigh Compton. Lady of the manor, estate owner, and chief administrator of the village of Sitting Marsh. As such, I have a certain authority—"

"Not when it comes to the business of the United States Army Air Force, you don't. Ma'am."

Elizabeth felt just a teensy bit irritated. "I would say that a dead body hanging from the bell rope in St. Matthews's bell tower is very definitely my business, since the incident happened in my village, so to speak."

The corporal continued to look unimpressed, much to Elizabeth's annoyance. "Ma'am, unless you're a member of the British police force, you're not coming in. Ma'am."

"But you can't refuse the lady of the manor—"

A muscle twitched in his cheek—the only movement

in his otherwise rigid face. "Ma'am, I wouldn't let you pass if you were the king of England."

"Well!" It was amazing how much exasperation one could put into that one word, Elizabeth thought, with a murderous glare. "Obviously you have no idea whom you are addressing. I shall simply have to talk to your superiors and inform them of your complete lack of co-operation and respect."

If the corporal was disturbed by her idle threat, he showed no sign. "Yes, ma'am."

Elizabeth did not like to be defeated. But then neither did she care to waste her breath on an argument she'd already lost. Turning her back on the infuriating man, she marched around the side of the bell tower and headed for the vicarage.

The Reverend Roland Cumberland was in the tiny front yard of his parochial home, snipping dead twigs off a rather sad-looking rosebush. "Not a good year for roses," he informed Elizabeth, after greeting her in a somewhat perfunctory manner.

Sensing he had something heavy on his mind, she chose her words carefully. "I see you have a visitor stationed at the bell tower."

The vicar nodded glumly. "Pesky American military police. Won't even let me go in there. How am I supposed to ring the bells for the evening service if I can't go into the bell tower? Last night I had only a handful of parishioners in the pews. Disgrace, that's what I call it."

Fully aware that on any given weeknight there were never more than a few dedicated worshipers in the church, Elizabeth did her best to look sympathetic. "It is a nuisance, I agree. Let's hope they soon finish whatever they are doing in there and leave us in peace."

The vicar raised his face to the sky. "Amen to that."

"I was wondering, Vicar. The night of the murder, you were at home, I presume?"

He dropped his chin, his eyes wary behind the thick lenses. "Yes, yes, of course. Asleep in my bed, naturally."

"Then you were not aware of anything unusual around the churchyard that night? You didn't hear anything? Anything at all? No footsteps, voices, creaking gates?"

The vicar pursed his lips. "Nothing. I'm fortunate to be blessed with the deep slumber of the righteous. Nothing disturbs me until morning. Unless I hear the bells ringing, of course." He looked a little uncomfortable. "Actually, it was Deirdre who heard them. She had to give me a little nudge. But I'm quite sure I would have awoken if she'd just given me a little longer."

"I'm sure you would have, Vicar." Elizabeth glanced at the reverend's quaint little house. "Is Deirdre at home, by any chance?"

The vicar frowned in concentration, then declared, "Gardening club. Then she'll be visiting hospital patients in North Horsham. You might catch her in Bessie's bakeshop around eleven or so. Though if you want to know if she heard anything, I can tell you now. She didn't. She would have told me. Deirdre never misses a thing, and never mises an opportunity to tell me about it. If she'd heard something unusual that night, she would have dragged me out of bed to investigate."

Elizabeth smiled at the vision of the sedate Deirdre Cumberland dragging her husband from his bed and shoving him outside in his pajamas. "Well, I won't keep you now, Vicar. But if you should remember anything, you will let me know, won't you?"

"Of course, Lady Elizabeth. But as I've told those American officers, I have no idea who might have done this terrible thing. If I had, I'd certainly want to see him face the consequences of such a dreadful deed. Taking the life of another is a deadly sin."

"It is indeed, Vicar. I think I'll just take a quick peek

around the churchyard before I leave. You never know what I might find."

The vicar gave her a shrewd look. "I think the American investigators have already confiscated anything that might be of interest. I appreciate your concern, Lady Elizabeth, but I must caution you about the dangers of participating in this nasty business."

Elizabeth waved an airy hand in dismissal. "Don't worry, Vicar. I know what I'm doing, and I promise I won't get in the way of that rude American in the bell tower."

She left the vicar snipping his rosebushes, and trod around the perimeter of the church and the grounds. After satisfying herself that there was nothing out of the ordinary to be found, she returned to her motorcycle and lifted the hem of her skirt to ease a leg over the seat.

It was a maneuver that had taken months of practice to manage gracefully, and even now, every time she climbed aboard, she shuddered to think what her mother would say if she knew that the sole heir to the Wellsborough estate was cavorting around the town perched on the seat of a motorcycle and sidecar.

The truth was, of course, that she could not afford a motorcar, and even if she could, she didn't know how to drive, which would mean hiring a chauffeur, since Violet had never been behind the wheel of anything mechanical, and half the time Martin wasn't even aware there was such a thing as a motorcar, much less how to drive one.

She arrived a short time later at the gate of Henrietta's cottage. Henrietta had leased the cottage at least a month ago, and Elizabeth was feeling rather guilty about not having visited the elderly lady before this. According to Violet, the widow had no family except for a grandson who lived in London.

As she marched up the pathway to the weather-beaten door, Elizabeth promised herself that she would remember to drop by more often to keep an eye on her newest tenant.

As she stepped up onto the tiny porch, she heard the shrill whistle of a teakettle. A moment later the sound was abruptly cut off, and Elizabeth smiled. It seemed as if she'd arrived at just the right time to enjoy a cup of tea. She lifted the brass lion's head that served as a door knocker and let it fall with a soft thud.

The door opened almost immediately, and a white-haired lady wrapped in a thick red shawl peered through a pair of metal frame glasses, with a worried look on her wrinkled face.

Elizabeth hurried to reassure her. "Mrs. Jones? I'm Lady Elizabeth from the Manor House. I brought you a few bits and pieces I thought you might find useful." She held out the basket to the old lady, who hesitated before she reached to take it.

Elizabeth saw her wince and said quickly, "Oh, I'm sorry, perhaps I should carry it in for you."

She flung out her hands but Henrietta hung on to the basket, answering in a low, husky voice that sounded like the effects of a bad cold. "It's very kind of you, I'm sure. I'm having a bit of trouble with my rheumatism right now. I get it in my elbows now and then. I was just in the kitchen, making a cup of tea. Would you care to join me?"

She turned and carried the basket across the tiny living room and through the door that led to the kitchen. Elizabeth stepped into the house and closed the front door behind her.

It had been some time since she had been inside the cottage. The last tenant had died and the house had been empty for months until the estate agent in North Horsham had informed Elizabeth that he'd leased it again.

Studying the faded wallpaper with a critical eye, she wondered if anyone had inspected the premises before Henrietta Jones moved in. That was the trouble with having to use an agent in North Horsham. He was too far away for constant supervision, and she knew from experience how lax the agents could be.

"You must let me know, Mrs. Jones," she called out, "if you have any repairs that need doing. As your landlord I'm responsible for the upkeep of the cottages." Which the rent hardly covers, she thought ruefully.

Henrietta didn't answer, but went on rattling cups in the kitchen.

Elizabeth went to the door and peered in. The old lady was carefully placing biscuits on a plate and seemed unaware that her visitor was right behind her. Deciding that the rheumatism wasn't preventing her hostess from managing the refreshments, Elizabeth returned to the living room and seated herself on a shabby settee in front of the fireplace.

A moment or two later Henrietta emerged from the kitchen awkwardly balancing a tray, which she set down on a footstool near Elizabeth's feet. The effort must have caused her pain after all, since she winced again.

"Oh, do let me pour," Elizabeth offered quickly, but Henrietta ignored her, and lifted the jug of milk to pour a small amount into the china cups.

Felling somewhat slighted, Elizabeth took the steaming cup and saucer from the old lady's shaking hand. "Thank you so much. How are you enjoying our little village? It must seem so quiet after living in London, though I suppose nowadays that's a good thing."

Henrietta looked up. "One lump or two, Lady Elizabeth?"

Elizabeth felt decidedly foolish. She had totally forgotten until that moment that Violet had told her Henrietta Jones was stone deaf. No wonder the poor woman hadn't answered her. She held up two fingers to indicate two lumps, then took a biscuit from the plate Henrietta offered her.

"Thank you," she said loudly, mouthing the words

with exaggeration so that Henrietta could understand. "This is very nice."

The old lady looked pleased. "I hope you like the biscuits, your ladyship."

Elizabeth took a small bite out of the biscuit, then exclaimed in surprise, "These are wonderful! What are these little round things imbedded in them? They taste like chocolate." She examined the biscuit closely before taking another bite, this time savoring the morsel before swallowing it. "It *is* chocolate. How divine! I've never seen anything like this before. Little chunks of chocolate inside a biscuit. Where did you get them? I must tell Violet about them. These are absolutely delicious."

Henrietta stared at her in confusion, and impatient with herself, Elizabeth tried again. She pointed at the biscuit, and rubbed her stomach with a rapturous look on her face.

Henrietta nodded, her face wreathed in smiles.

Elizabeth tried mouthing and using gestures, but she couldn't seem to make Henrietta understand that she wanted to know where she could buy the biscuits, and in the end she gave up. She thought about writing the question down for her, but Henrietta started talking about how much she appreciated the provisions and how difficult it was to get into town to shop, what with the bus stop being so far to walk and she didn't have a car, and even if she did, she couldn't drive it.

Elizabeth soon forgot about the biscuits in her efforts to make Henrietta understand that she would arrange for someone to take her into town once a week in order to get her shopping done.

In spite of her handicaps, Henrietta was a lively companion, and amazingly cheerful under the circumstances. Although she understood little of what Elizabeth tried to tell her, she rattled on about her experiences in the Blitz, during which she'd apparently lost her hearing when a bomb exploded just yards from her house.

By the time Elizabeth was ready to leave, she was full of admiration for the feisty old lady, and made up her mind that she would personally see that Henrietta got into town at least once a week.

As she stood to leave a flash of light from the mantelpiece caught her eye. Moving closer, she saw a pair of gold cufflinks, each with a tiny diamond in the corner. She picked one up to examine it, then put it down again when she realized Henrietta was watching her.

"Those are my grandson's," Henrietta explained in her raspy voice. "Charlie's been ever so good to me since my Albert died. Not many young men like him would bother with an old lady the way he does. Our Charlie has a heart of gold, bless him. Comes down every now and again to see me, he does. He's a good boy, is our Charlie."

Elizabeth smiled and nodded in agreement, then said good-bye to the charming little widow. "I'll be back soon, I promise," she told her, hoping Henrietta could understand. "I'll see if I can get Dr. Sheridan to bring you something for that rheumatism."

She wasn't sure if the old lady understood or not, but Henrietta nodded her head and thanked her profusely before closing the door.

Making her way back to her motorcycle, Elizabeth thanked her lucky stars that she was healthy, and prayed that the good Lord would see fit to allow her to stay that way for many years to come. She rode back to the manor at a leisurely pace, wondering how on earth she was going to get past the stony-faced American posted at the door of the bell tower.

CHAPTER

❦ 5 ❦

"Peaches?" Elizabeth exclaimed, when Violet put down the dessert plate in front of her. "Where on earth did you get peaches? I haven't seen a peach since before the rationing began."

"I don't like them," Martin mumbled, staring at his plate with deep suspicion. "Too much fuzz on the skin. I might as well be eating my dressing gown." He poked at the offending peach with his spoon. "Are you sure these are real? They look like ornaments, such as the wax apples on the sideboard."

Ignoring him, Violet grabbed a dish towel and began wiping the kitchen counter with it. "I don't remember where I got them. They were sitting in the larder and I thought you'd enjoy them with your lunch. Tell me how you got on with Henrietta Jones this morning. Didn't you have a hard time talking to her? I know I did—"

"Violet." Elizabeth gave her housekeeper's back a

hard stare. "Where did you get the peaches?"

Violet opened a cupboard door and banged it shut again. "Where does it matter where I got them from? Why can't you just enjoy them instead of worrying about things that don't concern you."

"This does concern me, Violet. It concerns me very much. Earl gave them to you, didn't he? I've told you again and again I won't have you accepting gifts from the Americans."

Violet swung around, eyes sparkling with fire. "Major Monroe did not give the peaches to me, Lizzie, so get off your high horse. Even if he did, I don't understand what you're making such a fuss about. If a gentleman is nice enough to give a lady a gift, the very least she can do is accept it with good grace."

"Speaking of Grace," Martin said, peering over the top of his spectacles, "there are puddles in the drawing room again."

Violet clicked her tongue. "I told Polly not to let them in there."

Elizabeth's lips tightened. "You know very well how I feel about accepting gifts from the Americans, Violet. I won't have people saying we're taking advantage of our guests just because they happen to be billeted at the Manor House. There is enough gossip going around as it is. You know how the villagers love to talk. After all, I have to set an example, or everyone would be grabbing everything they could get from the Americans. That's if they don't already."

"And just how are people going to find out what we do in our own home? Violet poked herself in the chest with her thumb. "I'm certainly not going to tell them."

"I should hope not!" Martin exclaimed. "What will people think if they heard that we have guests who use the drawing room for a bathroom?"

"You won't have to tell them anything," Elizabeth said dryly. "You can safely leave that to Polly. Where is she, anyway? I haven't seen her this morning."

"I sent her to clean the bathrooms. Bloody disgrace they are. She keeps whining that she doesn't have time to do them now that she's working in the office. I told her that the housework is supposed to be her first concern, and that she only helps out in the office if she has time after that."

"Perhaps that's why Grace doesn't use the bathroom," Martin observed. "It's not clean enough."

Violet finally lost her patience. "Will you listen to me for once, you silly old fool." She banged the table with her fist. "I keep telling you, George and Gracie are dogs, not people. Dogs, Martin. Animals with four legs that bark and pee around table legs."

Martin looked offended. "Well, why didn't you say so? I hope Polly gets it all cleaned up, or Grace will get the blame. Wouldn't do to offend our guests, you know."

Violet threw her hands up in despair and turned her back on him.

Elizabeth dug her spoon into a juicy peach, then lifted the dripping sliver to her mouth. It tasted every bit as wonderful as she remembered. For a moment she forgot she was supposed to be cross with Violet. "I suppose we should try to find someone to help out with the housework, now that Polly spends so much time in the office. I really can use her help. Things have been so much more organized since she started working in there."

"What surprises me is that anything Polly does is organized," Violet said crisply. "Anyhow, can we afford to hire someone else?"

Elizabeth made a face. "Not really. The money from the tour will help for a while, though, and by the time that's gone, I'll think of something else. I suppose I could have a go at cleaning the chimneys myself—"

Violet's shocked gasp interrupted her. "Elizabeth Hartleigh Compton, whatever next? You know very well you can't clean the chimneys. That's what we have chimney sweeps for."

"Quite right." Martin nodded his head in agreement.

"All of whom are serving in His Majesty's forces," Elizabeth reminded her.

"No, madam." Martin shook his head. "They are much too young to be serving in the forces. Though if you ask me, sending little children up into those sooty chimneys can't be much good for their health."

"They stopped doing that forty years ago." Violet rolled her eyes and shook her head at Elizabeth. "Getting worse, he is. Going blooming barmy, if you ask me."

Elizabeth glanced at Martin, who had apparently forgotten he didn't like peaches and was happily munching on the juicy, syrupy fruit.

"He seems perfectly fine to me."

"Well, don't expect him to help you sweep the chimneys, that's all I can say."

"We won't need his help. After all, how difficult can it be to sweep a chimney? We simply spread sheets over everything, push the brushes up the chimney and pull them down again. I've seen the sweeps do it plenty of times. It doesn't look that hard. Grubby perhaps, but Desmond can help us."

"Desmond is a gardener, not a sweep. He's not going to like being asked to mess about with the chimneys."

"Now that the summer is over, there isn't a lot to do in the grounds. He'll have plenty of time."

Violet tilted her head to one side. "And where, may I ask, are you going to get the brushes?"

Elizabeth waved a hand in dismissal. "Oh, Desmond will find some. He's very good at ferreting out all sorts of things."

"Ferrets?" Martin dropped his spoon in his plate. "I say, madam, you will have to be careful with those little perishers. They'll take a nip out of you as soon as look at you. I hope you're not going to let them run loose around the drawing room. Grace won't like that at all."

Elizabeth smiled at him and patted his hand. "Don't worry, Martin. We won't let anything loose in the drawing room." She pushed her chair back and stood. "I'll see if I can find Desmond and ask him about the chimney brushes, then I'm going to pop down to the cricket pavilion. I'd ask Polly to go, but since she's busy with the bathrooms, I'd better go myself. The sooner I get a list together of what needs to be done before the cricket match, the better."

Violet shook her head. "I still think you're crazy trying to get those Americans to play cricket. They are never going to beat our boys, then when our lads win, they'll crow over the Yanks and that'll start a fight and—"

"Crows now," Martin muttered. "We're turning the manor house into a zoo. The master is going to be most displeased about that. Most displeased."

Elizabeth sighed. "You worry far too much, Violet. I'm quite sure the men have learned their lesson after the fiasco at the town hall. They all got into so much trouble, they'll think twice before engaging in battle with one another again."

Violet sniffed. "Didn't stop them having a go at one another down the Tudor Arms on Saturday night, now did it?"

"I'm sure that was nothing compared to the one at the town hall." Elizabeth reached the door and looked back at her housekeeper. "Wait and see, Violet. The men will all be on their best behavior at the cricket match. I'm really quite sure of it."

She closed the door quickly, before Violet could answer with one of her sharp retorts. She wasn't about to let her housekeeper cast doubts on her great idea. The match had to be a success. It just had to, if they were ever going to have peace in the village between the Brit-

ish and the Americans. Dismissing her misgivings, she
went in search of Desmond.

The gardener was surprisingly eager to help with the
chimney sweeping project. He stood by the angel fountain on the back lawn, twisting his cap in his hands while
he listened intently against the noise of the cascading
water to Elizabeth's proposal.

"Well, I've never attempted to clean a chimney before," he said, when she was finished explaining what
she wanted, "but I think I know where I can get me
hands on some brushes. Just leave it to me, mum."

"Thank you so much," Elizabeth exclaimed, delighted
at how simple things were turning out. "Violet and I
would really appreciate any help you can give us. This
really is most generous of you, Desmond. It is so grat-
ifying to have help we can trust."

The gardener nodded, his craggy face turning pink
with the unexpected compliment. "My pleasure, m'm.
Don't you worry, now. We'll have these chimneys clean
in no time."

Relieved that everything had been so simple after all,
Elizabeth felt her confidence mounting as she rode her
motorcycle through the town. Several housewives in the
high street waved to her, heaving their loaded shopping
baskets onto one arm to free the other.

She waved back, feeling a sense of well-being. One
of the joys of her inheritance was the respectful recog-
nition she was given by the residents of Sitting Marsh.
She loved the village and its people. Her greatest pleasure in her work came when she was able to contribute
something toward their comfort and welfare. Now, if
only she could solve the murder case for Earl, she could
really enjoy the prospect of the cricket match.

The cricket pavilion was situated on the outskirts of
Sitting Marsh, on the edge of the woods. The field had
been sadly neglected in the past year, and would have

to be mowed before anyone could play a match on it.

She would have to discuss that with Desmond, Elizabeth reflected, as she climbed off her motorcycle. After tugging at her skirt to straighten it, she climbed the steps to the door of the pavilion.

The green walls of the long, wooden, rectangular building were desperately in need of paint. Elizabeth touched a dry, loose chip and watched it float to the floorboards. That was something they'd just have to live with for now, she decided. Moving on, she used the keys that had been in the councillors' possession ever since the pavilion had been closed down, and opened the door. With any luck the rooms would at least be salvageable.

At first the contrast from the pale sunlight outside blinded her, and she blinked several times before her eyesight gradually adjusted. Folding chairs had been stacked against the far wall, and a long trestle table graced another wall. At one end a pile of rubbish turned out to be American chewing gum wrappers and cigarette packages, empty beer bottles, and other remains left behind by visitors to the building.

The abandoned pavilion had earned a certain notoriety these days for being a lovers' rendezvous, as evidenced by the litter left around. When it came to passion, it seemed, locked doors were no match against the determination of the young. In fact, she noticed at least two windows that had been forced open, and did her best to secure them again.

Surprised to find the back room, which had once served as a storeroom, already unlocked, Elizabeth investigated, and was intrigued to spot wisps of green straw lying around on the floor. It looked as if the curly material could have been used for stuffing . . . perhaps for a toy or a pillow. Certainly she hadn't seen anything like it before.

After thoroughly inspecting the premises, she decided that with a thorough cleaning and a tablecloth or two to cover the scars on the table, the place could be made fairly presentable, after all.

As usual, Rita Crumm had offered the services of her long-suffering crew, and with the decorations rescued from the Town Hall Massacre, as some people called it, they might even achieve a semblance of festivity in the place.

Bessie had promised to donate refreshments from her bakeshop for a fraction of her usual fee, no doubt boosted by products smuggled out of the base by her generous American customers. In fact, Elizabeth decided, as she let herself out of the building and locked it again, she should drop in on Bessie and discuss the menu.

She was about to mount her motorcycle again when something caught her eye at the edge of the building. Just to make sure, she walked over to take a closer look. Strangely, she saw that the ridges she'd observed were actually heavy tire tracks, cut deep into the grass.

Someone had driven a lorry up onto the grass, possibly to hide it behind the pavilion out of sight. A rather large vehicle, judging from the depth of the tracks. Following them, Elizabeth discovered that the lorry had been parked behind the building, as she'd suspected. Shaking her head, she retraced her steps. Someone must have had a party in the pavilion. Probably more than one. And most likely the guest list had included a number of Americans, which would explain the lorry.

Making a mental note to get the windows repaired and locked right away, she rode back into town, her mouth watering at the thought of sampling some of Bessie's pastries.

As it happened, Rita Crumm sat in the corner of the charming little tearoom with two companions when Elizabeth arrived there a short while later. As she seated herself at her usual table, all three murmured a greeting, which she answered with a graceful raising of her hand.

The afternoon sun found its way through the small squares of the leaded pane window and cast an intricate pattern across the white tablecloth. It looked rather like a giant deformed checkerboard, Elizabeth mused, as she waited to be served. It had been so long since she'd played checkers. Her father had often challenged her to a game when she was growing up. How she missed him. And her mother.

Fortunately, just as she was beginning to feel sorry for herself, Bessie hustled over to the table, her plump face beaming. Normally she sent one of her girls to wait on tables, but Elizabeth always received personal service from Bessie herself. Elizabeth secretly maintained that Bessie used her as an excuse to sit out in the quiet elegance of the tearoom and enjoy her own baking, rather than any deference to her honored guest.

"I have just pulled a batch of scones from the oven, your ladyship," Bessie gushed, as Elizabeth removed her gloves. "If you'd care to wait a minute or two for them to cool, I could serve them with fresh Devonshire cream and some of my homemade strawberry jam."

Having had lunch not long before, Elizabeth wasn't exactly hungry, but the thought of Bessie's scones whetted her appetite. "That sounds marvelous, Bessie, thank you. Meanwhile, I wonder if you could spare a moment to discuss with me the menu for the cricket match?"

"Of course, m'm. If you'll just give me a minute in the kitchen."

She scuttled away, and a second or two later Rita Crumm's imperious voice rang out across the room. "Lady Elizabeth, am I to assume that the cricket match will be taking place quite soon?"

Elizabeth gritted her teeth. Trust Rita to conduct a conversation clear across the tearoom, rather than approach her as protocol demanded. She was tempted to ignore the woman, but she needed her services and that of her followers if the cricket match was to be a success.

Raising her voice just high enough to be heard, she announced, "The cricket match will take place a week from tomorrow, though we will be having a short rehearsal next Monday evening, to teach the Americans how to play the game."

"That'll be a laugh," Marge Gunther muttered. "I'll volunteer for that one."

Nellie Smith, the only unmarried woman at the table, tittered and dug her elbow into the plump woman's side.

Rita managed to freeze both women with a single glance. "I see. Then we shall need to get the place spruced up some time this week."

"If you would be so kind." Elizabeth managed the semblance of a smile. The feud between herself and Rita Crumm was a bitter one. Everyone in the village was aware that Elizabeth's father had married beneath him. His wife had been nothing more than a kitchen maid when Lord Wellsborough met and married her. The fifteen-year-old bride had spent her life trying to live down her humble beginnings, and society being what it was, had unwittingly handed the stigma down to her daughter.

Elizabeth had managed to rise above the blot on her lineage, and for the most part, the villagers appeared to have forgotten about it. There were one or two, however, who still resented the fact that the illustrious position of lady of the manor and custodian of Sitting Marsh had been handed to the daughter of a common servant. Rita Crumm was one such person.

Rita seemed to spend a vast amount of time doing her best to better Elizabeth's efforts. Then again, Rita spent most of her time proving to everyone that she could surpass anyone else on the entire earth. Elizabeth was not one to refuse a challenge, and therefore her relationship with her formidable opponent more often than not resulted in a battle of wits.

At that moment, Elizabeth was trying to repress her

resentment at having to ask a favor of her sworn enemy. It made her feel only slightly better to open her handbag, lay the keys to the pavilion on the tablecloth, and say sweetly, "Here are the keys, Rita. You can pick them up on the way out."

Rita lifted her chin, then glared at Nellie. "Don't just sit there. Go and fetch the keys for me. Please."

Nervous Nellie had not earned her nickname for nothing. She leaped to her feet, sending her chair crashing back into the one behind it in her haste to retrieve the keys.

Feeling sorry for her, Elizabeth dropped them into the woman's trembling hand.

"Thank you, your ladyship," Nellie whispered, and scampered back to her table, just as Bessie reappeared with a tray of scones and a silver teapot.

"Now then, Lady Elizabeth," Bessie announced, as she poured the steaming brown liquid into the cup, "if you would care to discuss the menu, I have a few minutes to spare. If I may join you?"

"Of course." Elizabeth gave the pink-cheeked woman a warm smile. "I'll enjoy the company."

"Thank you, your ladyship." Bessie dropped onto the chair with a sigh of relief. "I'm getting too old to be on my feet all day, that I am. I keep thinking it's time I sold the bakeshop and took a rest."

Elizabeth looked at her in alarm. "Don't say that, Bessie. Sitting Marsh wouldn't be the same without your wonderful cakes and pastries to enjoy. The bakeshop is as much an institution in the village as is St. Matthew's."

Bessie chuckled. "Well, thank you, your ladyship. That's always nice to hear." She shot a glance at the table in the corner, where Rita appeared to be deep in conversation with her companions. Leaning forward, she whispered, "Speaking of the church, any news on who might have killed that poor boy in the bell tower?"

Keeping her voice just as low, Elizabeth answered,

"Not yet, though I understand the American investigators are looking into it."

"I know." Bessie helped herself to a scone and split it expertly with her knife. "They were in here, asking questions. Of course, no one knew anything. Most of us didn't even know the young man. Though I think Ted and Alfie, down at the pub, knew who he was. Troublemaker, so I heard. Still, he didn't deserve to be murdered like that. All that way from home, too. His poor parents."

"Yes, indeed," Elizabeth murmured, busy calculating if she had time to get down to the Tudor Arms to talk to Ted and Alfie and still be back at the Manor House in time for dinner.

"Well, about this menu," Bessie announced, raising her voice so heartily, she made Elizabeth jump. "I thought ham, sausages and cheese, some of my home-baked, bread, pickles, jelly, blancmange and trifle, and of course pastries. I thought I'd make cherry cakes, and fruit flans as well."

Elizabeth stared at her in amazement. "How are you going to manage all that on your rations?"

"Ah, that would be telling, wouldn't it. Don't you worry, your ladyship, I'll give those Yanks a feast to remember. That's a promise."

Elizabeth frowned. She knew better than to pry, but it concerned her that Bessie was so confident about her ability to conjure up such a sumptuous spread. "Speaking of good food, I ran across something this morning that I hadn't seen before. Little round pieces of chocolate imbedded in a biscuit. Very tasty. I was wondering if you'd seen them anywhere."

"Oo, yes, m'm. They're called chocolate chips. Made in America, they are. They have them on the base. It's amazing how chocolate tastes all the better when it's off ration."

Bessie laughed heartily, but Elizabeth didn't feel like

joining in. She was becoming increasingly uncomfortable with this sudden excess of food supposedly in short supply. It would seem that a great many people were benefitting from what appeared to be an endless stream of black market goods.

Surely they couldn't have that many contacts on the base. There had to be a source of supply somewhere in the village, which would be highly illegal, of course. Someone in Sitting Marsh was breaking the law, and it was up to her to find that person before he or she got everyone else into trouble.

Anxious now to get on with her itinerary, she finished her scone and the last of her tea, then bade Bessie goodbye. With some reluctance, she paused at Rita's table on the way out. "I appreciate you ladies taking the trouble to clean up the pavilion for the cricket match," she told them, managing to avoid looking at Rita directly.

"We'll be happy to do it, your ladyship," Marge chirped. "Makes a change, doesn't it."

"We ladies of the Housewives League are always happy to do what we can for the troops, your ladyship," Rita added. "Besides, it'll be worth it for the fun of watching those Yanks make fools of themselves."

Elizabeth's smile froze. "I wouldn't be too sure of that if I were you, Rita. The Americans have a habit of turning the tables on us all. It could very well be our British soldiers who will be the ones to look the fools."

She marched out of the bakeshop before Rita could think of a suitable retort. Right now she had more important things to do than argue with someone whose judgment was based solely on her need to outshine everyone and everything.

Right now she needed to talk to Ted and Alfie and find out what they knew about Kenny Morris. As for the mystery of the black market goods, she'd simply have to take care of that later. After all, this business of murder was far more important than a few boxes of contraband smuggled out of the base. Dismissing the problem from her mind, she headed for the Tudor Arms.

CHAPTER

❧ 6 ❧

Polly sat back on her heels and wiped the beads of perspiration from her forehead with the back of her arm. Housework certainly took the chill out of her bones, even though the house felt as cold as a morgue. Not that she'd ever been in a morgue.

Shivering at the thought, Polly cast one critical glance over the gleaming bathtub and climbed to her feet. At least the loo was clean for a while. Her lips twitched in amusement. She'd only just started calling the bathroom a loo, since Marlene had read about the new word in one of the magazines she kept in the hairdresser's where she worked.

Violet never knew what it meant, and Polly got the biggest delight out of using the word. It wasn't often she got one over on Violet. Polly picked up her bucket and mop and trudged wearily out of the bathroom. What with the dusting and polishing, window cleaning and black-leading the grates in the massive fireplaces, she'd had no time to do her work in the office. There wasn't enough time to do both jobs. Her ladyship would just have to hire someone else to do the housework, that's all. She'd ask her about it the first chance she got.

Deep in thought about where her replacement might be found, she barely registered the sound of heavy footsteps marching down the wide hallway that led to the great hall. By the time she did, it was almost too late to hide the bucket and mop and whip off her apron.

The only reason she'd started work in the office at all was because she'd lied to Sam about being Lady Elizabeth's secretary to impress him. Well, after that, she'd had to make it come true, hadn't she. After all, she could hardly let Sam know she was only a housemaid. Of course, she'd lied about her age, too, but she couldn't do anything about that. The only real problem she'd had was hiding from Sam and the rest of the GIs while she was doing the housework. All the boys knew about her and Sam, and they were bound to tell him if they caught her cleaning the loo.

Luckily, she was inches away from a suit of armor standing in the corner by one of the enormous windows. She'd barely shoved everything behind it when the footsteps turned the corner and three men came into view.

Polly's first thought was how lucky she'd been. One of the men was Sam, and he was heading straight toward her. As usual, her stomach flipped at the sight of him in the forest green uniform that was so much more glamorous than the baggy khaki uniforms the British soldiers wore.

The next second she realized something was wrong. Although Sam was only feet away now, he acted as if he hadn't seen her. He was staring straight ahead, his face as gloomy as the statue of the Roman gladiator on the back terrace. Her gaze slid to the men on either side of him, and now her stomach seemed to drop to her knees. No wonder Sam was looking grim. The men were military policemen, and they had him by the arms.

With a little cry she shot forward. "Sam! What's happening? Where are they taking you?"

He flicked a glance at her, a look so full of despair, she felt sick. Running to keep up with the three men, her throat closed and her voice cracked when she tried to speak again. "Sam?"

He gave her a slight shake of his head, and one of the MPs said sharply, "This man is under arrest. Please stay out of our way."

"Under arrest? No! What for? You can't arrest him. He's done nothing bad."

Sam spoke then, his voice so cold, it froze her heart. "Go away, Polly. Leave me alone."

Polly stood stock-still in the middle of the great hall, watching the man she adored being marched through the door and out of sight. Then, with one hand over her mouth to stifle her sobs, she fled to the kitchen.

Inside the Tudor Arms, Elizabeth was surprised to see the evening crowd already beginning to build up. A group of locals sat in the corner of the lounge bar, chased out of the public bar, no doubt, by a bunch of rowdy American airmen playing a boisterous game of darts.

Alfie, the bartender, raised his hand in a salute as Elizabeth approached the counter. Two young British soldiers turned their heads to glance at her, then went back to their beer.

"Good evening, Alfie." Elizabeth perched on one of the bar stools and tried to look as if she belonged there. Thanks to her upbringing, she still felt terribly out of place on the rare occasion she visited the Tudor Arms. Her father would be enraged to know she set foot in such a place, much less accepted the free glass of sherry Alfie slipped her.

But then again, this ancient building with its low, heavily beamed ceilings and stone walls had seen many changes over the centuries. Although this era in particular was probably the most startling, what with American servicemen taking over the public bar, women frequenting the place as often as the men, and the lady of the manor sipping sherry at the lounge bar alongside two privates in His Majesty's army. Times had changed, indeed.

After enjoying a sip or two, she took advantage of the lull in customers and beckoned to Alfie.

He hurried over at once. "Is everything all right, your ladyship? Sherry to your liking?"

At the mention of her title, the two soldiers sent curious glances her way. She pretended not to notice. "The sherry is wonderful, Alfie, as usual," she assured him. "You must get me a bottle or two of that brand the next time you order."

"I'll try, m'm," Alfie said, looking worried. "But you know how things are. Wartime, you know. Hard to get the stuff anymore. We haven't had a bottle of brandy in here since last Christmas."

Alfie's comment was obviously for the benefit of the two soldiers seated at the bar, since Elizabeth knew very well that he kept a bottle or two under the counter for his special customers.

"I know," she said solemnly. "Dreadful war. Still, one has to make sacrifices, I suppose."

"We do, indeed, m'm. Still, it's nothing compared to the sacrifices young men like these two have to make." He nodded his head at the soldiers, who immediately looked embarrassed. "Tell you what," he said to them, "why don't you take your beer over to that table over there, and I'll bring you a drop of whiskey to wash it down. On the house."

The soldiers looked surprised, but scrambled off their stools and headed for the table.

"Thank you, Alfie," Elizabeth said warmly. "I did rather want to talk to you in private."

Alfie nodded. "I knew that's what you wanted. If you'll just hang on a minute, your ladyship, I'll be right back."

She waited for him while he took the whiskey over to the soldiers. Someone in the public bar had begun pounding on the piano—loudly and quite badly. A deep voice bellowed out the latest war song, and soon the rest of his companions had joined in.

No longer concerned about being overheard, Elizabeth wasted no time in asking Alfie about Kenny Morris. According to the obliging bartender, the fight with Sam Cutter wasn't the first Kenny had been involved in at the pub.

"Bloody troublemaker, he was," Alfie said, busily polishing a glass tankard with a small yellow cloth. "Knew it the first time he came down. I told Ted, I did. That lad's going to end up in trouble, I said. Just you wait and see." He nodded slowly up and down. "And I was bloomin' right."

"You were, indeed," Elizabeth agreed. "I don't suppose you remember who else the young man fought with before his encounter with Sam Cutter?"

Alfie raised his chin and closed his eyes. "Can't think right now, m'm. There's been so many down here. I think it were with some of them English blokes, though. Not local, mind. Most of them what fight are soldiers from the camp in Beerstowe, or down from the Smoke. That's where them two came from." He nodded at the table with the soldiers. "Down from London this morning."

Elizabeth shook her head in amazement. "What brings soldiers all the way down here from London? There must be plenty of quiet places for a drink closer to the city."

"It's the American base, m'm. Wherever there are

Americans, there are girls. That's what the blokes are looking for. Hoping for the leftovers, I suppose, seeing as how the Yanks always get the first pick."

"Oh, dear," Elizabeth murmured. "No wonder there are so many hostilities between them."

"You're right, there. Though in the case of that Morris chap, it weren't so much fighting over the women with him. He was just a nasty piece of work, that's all. Though I do believe it was a girl what started his last fight, funny enough." He slid a wary glance at Elizabeth, who interpreted the reason right away.

"It's all right, Alfie. I know Sam was trying to protect Polly. She told me."

"Oh, well, that's all right, then." Alfie hung the tankard on a hook above his head. "I wouldn't want Polly to think I was the one what spilled the beans. She's got a lot of spirit, that girl. And a temper to match, so I've heard."

Elizabeth wondered if Alfie knew that Polly was only fifteen. It seemed a little late to worry about that now, especially since her sixteenth birthday was just a few weeks away, in which case she would be legally allowed to drink in the pub. "Well, I must be going," she said, sliding off her stool. "If you should hear anything more about Kenny that you think might be useful, I'd appreciate it if you would give me a ring at the house."

Alfie nodded. "Will do, your ladyship. Though I reckon them American investigators know a lot more than we do. Maybe you should ask them."

"I don't think they are likely to tell me anything," Elizabeth said with a smile. "Thank you so much for the excellent sherry, Alfie."

"My pleasure, m'm. Come again soon."

She slipped out of the door, thankful to breathe the clean, fresh air from the ocean. The smoke inside the pub was thick enough to choke her, and irritated her throat. Thank goodness she had never been tempted to try a cigarette. Neither Violet nor Martin had ever smoked, though her father had enjoyed a pipe now and then. Since he'd been gone, the library and study had smelled considerably fresher, though Elizabeth had often detected the smell of tobacco in the great hall, even before the Americans moved in.

Perhaps Polly had taken up the habit, or maybe the ghost Martin was always talking about smoked a pipe. The thought made Elizabeth uncomfortable. She didn't, for one minute, believe that Martin actually saw the ghost of her father walking the great hall, as he'd claimed so often, but there had been a time or two when she had felt an intense chill, even a strange presence up there that she'd found impossible to explain.

Roaring up the hill on her motorcycle toward the Manor House, she chided herself for her fanciful thoughts. She was allowing Martin's ramblings to influence her, she decided. Of course it was chilly in the great hall. It was cold everywhere in the house these days. The kitchen was the only cozy place in the entire building.

She could put it off no longer. The day after tomorrow, she would tackle the chimneys and get them swept. That having been decided, she sailed up the long, winding, tree-lined driveway to the mansion, wondering what illicit nourishment could possibly be waiting for her in Violet's well-stocked kitchen.

As usual, Martin took forever to respond after she'd tugged on the bellpull. Finally the solid oak door swung inward on its heavy iron hinges, as if pulled by an invisible hand. Peering into the dark hallway, Elizabeth said tentatively, "Martin?"

His muffled voice came from behind the door. "One moment, madam. I can't find my glasses."

"They are probably on your head," Elizabeth said, as she stepped inside. "That's where they usually are when you can't find them." Not that he needed them, since he never looked through them, anyway. She'd wasted her breath too many times reminding him of that fact.

"Bless my soul, indeed they are." The door began to close while Martin clung to the handle and shuffled to keep up with it. "I'm very glad you are home, madam. There has been all sorts of trouble since you left."

"Trouble?" Elizabeth unpinned her hat and handed it to him. "What kind of trouble?"

Martin stood looking at the hat as if he'd never seen one before.

Sighing, she took it from him and hung it on the hall stand. "Perhaps I'd better ask Violet." A sudden thought struck her and she looked at Martin in alarm. "Is something the matter with Violet?"

Martin looked surprised. "Violet? No, madam. The last time I saw her, she was her usual rambunctious self."

Elizabeth relaxed.

"Polly is somewhat distressed, though."

"Polly?"

"Yes, madam."

"What's the matter with Polly?"

"That I couldn't say, madam."

Elizabeth turned to head for the stairs.

"Some disaster with the Americans, I believe."

With a cold chill of apprehension Elizabeth ran lightly down the steps and along the hall to the kitchen.

She heard Polly wailing well before she threw open the door. The girl sat on a chair by the fireplace, weeping into a large handkerchief, while Violet stood at the stove, pouring boiling water into a large china teapot.

She looked up as Elizabeth burst into the room. "Oh, there you are, Lizzie," she said, apparently forgetting she wasn't supposed to be using the childhood name in front of Polly. "Thank goodness you're back. Maybe you can do something with her." She nodded at Polly, who sat hugging herself and rocking back and forth.

"Whatever is the matter?" Elizabeth patted Polly's shoulder and studiously avoided the first question that came to mind. She asked the next obvious one instead. "Has something happened to your father?" Polly's father was somewhere overseas in the army. There had been far too many of the dreaded telegrams arriving lately.

Polly shook her head, and uttered a shuddering sob.

"It's that young man she's so barmy about," Violet said, carrying a steaming mug over to the shivering girl.

"Sam Cutter?" The growing feeling of dread swelled to a tide of terror. She was terrified to ask, but she had to know. "Was he shot down? Do they have any news? Do you know who was with him?"

Polly put the mug down on the hearth, swallowed hard, and stammered, "No, m'm, he's not shot down or nothing. He was here a little while ago." She struggled to contain another sob, but her words came out on a wail, anyway. "He's been *arrested!*" A burst of fresh weeping followed her startling remark.

Still shaking from the fright of thinking Earl might have gone down with Sam Cutter in his plane, it took a moment or two for Elizabeth to understand what Polly had said.

Violet's tongue clicked with indignation as she poured another cup of tea. "I knew it was a mistake to take in those Americans. Harboring a murderer in the Manor House, indeed. Your parents would turn in their grave, not to mention having my guts for garters for letting you get yourself into this kind of trouble."

Ignoring Violet for the moment, Elizabeth cleared her mind. "Sam Cutter has been arrested? Why? On what charge?"

Polly choked and spluttered, and finally found her voice again. "They think he killed Kenny Morris."

Elizabeth looked at Violet, who shrugged. "I saw Major Monroe in the hall, and asked him why they'd taken the young man away. He told me Sam Cutter was being held on the base on suspicion of murder."

"I don't believe it. Did Earl say why they think the squadron leader killed Kenny Morris?"

"Ask Polly. She knows why."

Polly stopped crying and dashed away her wet tears. "He didn't do it, m'm, I just know he didn't. He was gambling that night with Kenny and some other blokes . . . and they all lost a lot of money and Kenny started a fight 'cos he said the dealer was cheating and Kenny and Sam got into it 'cos Sam was mad at Kenny and then Kenny broke a beer bottle and Sam cut his hand. He had it all bandaged up the next day and I asked him about it and that's when he told me what happened." She stared up at Elizabeth with puffy, red-rimmed eyes. "It's the truth, m'm, I know it. My Sam wouldn't hurt no one. Honest he wouldn't."

Elizabeth took a moment to sort through Polly's disjointed sentences. Finally she said slowly, "The police think Sam cut his hand with the knife that was dropped when Kenny was killed, is that it?"

Polly uttered yet another shuddering sigh. "I s'pose so, m'm." She started wailing again. "Oh, what am I going to do? I can't stand the thought of him being arrested and sent back to the States, I really can't."

Violet rolled her eyes at the ceiling.

"Well, first you'll drink your tea," Elizabeth said crisply, "then you are going home. There's nothing that you can achieve by sitting here crying, and your mother will be getting worried. We'll just have to see what we can do in the morning. Until then, you must do your best not to worry. I'm sure everything can be straightened out."

"I can't stop worrying," Polly wailed.

"Yes, you can, my girl," Violet said, stooping to retrieve the mug from the hearth. "Here, drink up. Then get yourself home before your mother starts calling here looking for you."

Polly obediently sipped the tea, pausing every now and then to utter a dry sob.

"When did they take Sam away?" Elizabeth asked, addressing Violet.

"About an hour ago." Violet reached for a cup and saucer in the cupboard. "Polly saw him being led out. She's been in hysterics ever since."

"I'm all right now." Although still white-faced, Polly managed to sound more like her old self when she added, "I'll be getting along now, your ladyship. Thank you."

"Don't worry, Polly." Elizabeth patted the girl on the shoulder. "I'll call the base first thing in the morning."

"You won't have to," Violet said grimly. "Major Monroe told me the American investigators will be here tomorrow to question everyone. Not that any of us can tell them anything, except Polly, that is."

Polly looked as if she would burst into tears again, and Elizabeth said hurriedly, "I promise, Polly, I won't let them question you without me being there."

"Thank you, m'm." Polly walked a little shakily to the door and disappeared.

Violet opened the oven door, emitting the most heavenly aroma. "Do you think he did it?"

Elizabeth suddenly realized she was hungry, after all. For a while there she'd lost her appetite. "I sincerely hope not, for Polly's sake. I don't know the young man very well. Did Earl—Major Monroe give any indication how he felt about it?"

"He sounded really disgusted, but he didn't say one way or the other what he thought about it." Violet pulled a bubbling casserole dish from the oven and set it on top of the stove. She peered at it closely for a moment or two, then said warily, "I think it's done."

"What is it?" Elizabeth asked, unable to contain her curiosity any longer.

"It's an American recipe," Violet said, sounding defensive. "One of the officers gave it to me. Chicken and dumplings. He said it's his mother's favorite recipe. I thought if we had some left over, I'd send up a plate for him."

Elizabeth tried not to smile. "I thought we weren't going to feed the Americans. Wasn't it you who said how impossible it would be to feed all those extra mouths with everything on ration? I seem to remember you mentioning something about the Americans probably wanting you to kill a cow."

Violet shrugged her thin shoulders. "That was before."

"Before what?"

"Before . . . never you mind."

Elizabeth was tempted to keep asking questions, but she wisely refrained. Somehow she had the idea she might not like the answers.

The chicken tasted as excellent as it smelled, though Martin spent some time prodding the dumplings before trusting himself to eat one. The meal was more peppery than they were accustomed to, and Martin swallowed three glasses of water while devouring his food, but for once he uttered not one complaint about Violet's cooking. In fact, he wore a very satisfied expression on his face when he dabbed his mouth with his serviette for the last time.

Violet watched him expectantly, though she should have known that waiting for a compliment from Martin was as fruitless as waiting for her hair to turn black again.

As for Elizabeth, apart from a delighted murmur of appreciation at the beginning of the meal, she made no further comment. She was too busy worrying about the coming interview with the American investigators. She would have liked to talk to Earl before they arrived, but it was too late now. He would have already retired to his room, and she could hardly pay him a visit there. She could only hope that Polly wouldn't say anything that might make matters worse, though at this moment, it didn't seem as if things could be much worse for Sam Cutter.

CHAPTER

❀ 7 ❀

The following morning Polly arrived at the Manor House with the haggard appearance of someone who hadn't had a wink of sleep all night. Observing the dark circles under her secretary's eyes, Elizabeth decided she needed something to make her feel better.

"I've been thinking, Polly," she said, as she helped the girl sort through the morning post. "Nowadays it seems that I spend more time out of the office than in it, which means there's a lot more work for you to do now. It might be a good idea to hire someone else to do the housework, and that will give you more time to get the work done in here."

Much to her dismay, instead of making Polly more cheerful, her announcement produced more tears. "That would be wonderful, your ladyship," the young girl said, her voice trembling with emotion.

"Of course, if you'd rather do the housework," Elizabeth assured her, feeling confused, "I can always find someone to help out in the office."

"Oh, no, m'm, no." Polly sniffed and hunted for the handkerchief she'd tucked up the sleeve of her red cardigan. "I just love working in the office, that's all. It's been my dream. I'm just so happy I don't have to do housework no more . . ." She burst into tears, and sobbed into her handkerchief.

Elizabeth was at a bit of a loss as to how to handle such hysterics. She sat down opposite the girl and covered one of her trembling hands with her own. "Polly, I don't think it's good for you to get yourself so upset about this business with Sam Cutter. After all, he is an American, and sooner or later he will be returning to his own country." Maybe sooner, she thought, if he's convicted of murder. She didn't voice that thought to Polly, however.

"Yes, m'm." Polly blew her nose loudly. "It's just that I know he didn't do it but I don't know who did and it looks like he'll get the blame and I can't do nothing to help him and I keep thinking it's my fault because he had that fight in the pub and I don't know what to do-hoo-hoo!"

Elizabeth waited until the burst of weeping had subsided before saying gently, "Polly, whatever went on in that bell tower, whether Sam had anything to do with it or not, had nothing to do with you. You can rest assured you are in no way to blame for what happened."

Polly appeared unconvinced. "I'm scared about what them investigators are going to ask. What if I get him into more trouble? I'd never forgive myself. He'd never forgive me. Oh, Lady Elizabeth, do I have to talk to them?"

"Yes, I'm afraid you do." Elizabeth sighed. "I know it can be scary, Polly, but just remember, you must tell the truth. Even if it seems that you might get Sam into trouble. If you don't tell the truth, you could both be in a lot more trouble later on."

"I know, m'm. That's what me mum and Marlene told me. Just tell the truth."

Relieved that the girl had confided in her family, Elizabeth was about to ask how they felt about Sam when the shrill ring of the phone cut her off. Startled, she jumped nearly as violently as Polly.

Polly stared at her, her eyes looking huge and black in her white face.

"Perhaps I should take that." Elizabeth stretched out her hand but Polly snatched at the receiver.

"No, m'm. It's my job." Putting on her best accent, she said politely into the mouthpiece, "This is the Manor House, and this is Lady Elizabeth's secretary speaking."

Any other day Elizabeth would have smiled at the transformation, but she was far too tense right now to enjoy Polly's metamorphosis. Instead, she waited, watching the young girl's face as she listened to the voice on the other end of the line.

"Yes, sir," Polly said finally. "I'll inform Lady Elizabeth. Thank you very much." She hung the receiver back on its rest, then said in a voice that barely trembled, "That was one of the investigators from the base. They'll be here this afternoon."

Elizabeth nodded. "Good. That will give me time to run an errand this morning. Meanwhile, the rents have to be entered into the book, and there are still some to be collected. If you feel like some fresh air, I could give you a lift in the sidecar and let you off in the village. You can collect the rents on the list while I take care of my business, then I'll pick you up on my way back."

Polly looked as if she'd been handed a reprieve from a prison sentence. "That would be smashing, Lady Elizabeth. Thank you. I'll get my coat."

"Right. Then meet me outside on the steps. I'll have Desmond fetch the motorcycle from the stables."

Happy that she'd brought a smile to the poor child's face, Elizabeth retrieved her coat and hat from the hall stand. She was winding her scarf around her neck when Martin appeared at the top of the stairs, wheezing and gasping for breath.

"Why didn't you wait for me, madam," he complained, between gasps for air. "I should be fetching your coat for you."

"Well, you are here now," Elizabeth said soothingly. "You can open the door for me."

"Yes, madam." Still looking affronted, Martin pulled open the door.

Elizabeth paused on the step, deciding she had better warn Martin of the forthcoming events. "We will be cleaning the chimneys tomorrow, Martin. That's if Desmond has managed to get hold of some brushes."

"Yes, madam."

"And there will be a Stately Homes tour on Saturday."

Martin blinked. "You are going on a tour, madam?"

"No, Martin. People will be coming here to tour the house."

"Oh, no, madam, that won't do. The master won't like that at all."

"The master is dead, Martin. I doubt if he'll complain." Elizabeth stepped outside and lifted her face into a light breeze that smelled of dying leaves and damp grass.

"He'll complain to me." Martin shuffled into the doorway and looked accusing. "He always complains to me. He doesn't like all these strange people in the house. Not to mention all the animals running around."

Stabbed by an unusual bout of irritation, Elizabeth said sharply, "Well, he'll just have to put up with it, won't he. If he hadn't been foolish enough to insist on going to a concert in London in the middle of the Blitz, he'd be alive now to take care of things. And so would my mother."

Martin's face closed up like the visor on a suit of armor. "Yes, madam."

Immediately contrite, Elizabeth touched Martin's wrinkled hand. "I'm sorry, Martin. To be perfectly honest, I don't care for strangers roaming around the Manor House, either. I wish there were some other way to find the money we need, but right now I can't think of one. Just try to put up with it, there's a dear. Violet will be escorting them around, and all you have to do is stay out of their way. Polly has promised to help, so everything should go quite smoothly."

"If you say so, madam."

He still wore his hurt expression, and Elizabeth descended the stone steps with a heavy heart. Poor Martin seemed to slip further and further into senility with every passing week. His insistence that the ghost of her father walked the great hall was the most disturbing of his delusions, and one that played on her mind a great deal.

The untimely death of her parents had devastated everyone and, as their only child, Elizabeth most of all. But there was no doubt in her mind that Martin missed her father even more than she did, which explained his hallucinations of Lord Wellsborough's ethereal return to his ancestral home.

She could only hope that the rumors went no further than the walls of the Manor House. Already some of the American officers had mentioned seeing apparitions in the great hall, though Elizabeth was inclined to think that such sightings had been manifested by a combination of beer, the eerie sound of noisy water pipes, and Martin's habit of confiding in anyone who would listen.

Another indication of Martin's failing mind, she thought soberly. There was a time when wild elephants wouldn't have dragged the slightest hint of such nonsense from his lips.

Polly burst out of the front door just as Elizabeth reached the bottom step. She leaped down the steps with such speed, Elizabeth was certain the young girl would plunge headfirst to the ground, but she landed lightly on her feet with an agility that Elizabeth envied with all her heart.

Although barely past thirty, she was beginning to feel the constraints of reaching her third decade, though she did her best to remain agile. Romping with the puppies helped, and no doubt the energy involved in the chimney sweeping would test her muscles, she thought wryly.

Shading her eyes with her hand, she surveyed the wide landscape of the Manor House grounds. Rolling lawns led down to a thick green fringe of trees that edged the woods. On one side a tall, prickly hedge hid the large plot where Desmond tended to the vegetables.

The residents of the Manor House had always enjoyed their own homegrown vegetables, centuries before the victory gardens had become essential to the war effort. Nowadays, however, the vegetable garden helped a great deal toward lightening the household bills.

"I don't see Desmond anywhere," Elizabeth said, squinting against the morning sun. "Do you see him, Polly?"

"No, your ladyship. I can't see him at all." Polly had crammed her long dark hair into a bright red woolly beret, which she'd pulled down low on her forehead in anticipation of the drafty ride into town. She reminded Elizabeth of the pictures of evacuees in the newspaper. The poor children had been pushed out of their London homes and deposited with strangers in the country in the interests of their safety.

Judging from some of the stories Elizabeth had heard, even if they were embellished by the press, some of those children would have been safer dodging the bombs at home. She had been struck by the look of abject misery on the faces of the little ones. Polly wore that look right now.

That worried Elizabeth a great deal. The child was far

too immature to be deeply attached to any young man, much less one who was considerably older than she, lived on the other side of the world, and at the moment was being held on suspicion of murder. She would have a long talk with her protégée, she decided. Though not right now.

"We had better fetch the motorcycle ourselves." Elizabeth fastened the top button of her coat. "It will be quicker than looking for Desmond. Besides, once he starts talking, it's hard to get rid of him."

"Yes, m'm." Polly trudged along at her side, head down. She seemed to have forgotten her momentary pleasure at being promoted to rent collector.

Elizabeth did her best to cheer her up. "The tour on Saturday should be rather fun, I think, showing off the Manor House. You and Violet should enjoy that."

"Yes, m'm. I just hope I can get it all clean by then."

Elizabeth felt a stab of guilt. She had put an awful lot on the shoulders of the young girl lately. "Polly, I promise you I will try to find someone to help out, at least until I can find someone permanent. It's so terribly difficult to find servants these days."

"Yes, m'm." Polly was quiet for a moment, and only the sound of their footsteps crunching on gravel disturbed the twittering of the birds above their heads. Then Polly burst out, "Maybe if you didn't call them servants, m'm, someone might be more inclined to take the job."

Astonished, Elizabeth stopped short. "Honestly? Are people really that sensitive nowadays?"

Polly stared at her boots. "Yes, m'm. That's what I think anyway. I never liked being called a servant, even though I am one, I suppose."

"Oh, dear." Elizabeth stared at her. "Is that why you wanted to work in the office, so that I wouldn't call you a servant?"

Polly looked up then, her cheeks pink with embarrassment. "Oh, no, m'm. It weren't that at all. I didn't really mind doing the housework, and I do love working in the office, honest I do. It's what I always wanted. It's just that nowadays the girls don't like being called servants. It makes them feel . . . well, sort of cheap, if you know what I mean." Her blush deepened. "Not that I think working at the Manor House is cheap, m'm, I just . . ." Her voice trailed off, and she traced a path in the gravel with the toe of her boot.

"I think I know exactly what you mean," Elizabeth said quietly. "And you are right, Polly. Young women today have so many more opportunities open to them. Especially now, with all our men away from home fighting the war and women taking over their jobs. If I want to hire someone to help Violet with the housework, I shall have to make the job sound more appealing. What do you suggest? The trouble is, I can't afford to pay them much."

Polly looked so pleased that she was being consulted, Elizabeth congratulated herself. "Well," she said slowly, "I think if you were to offer the job to the women in London with room and board, I think they'd shove each other out the way to get down here just to be near the Yanks."

"Oh, my." Elizabeth clutched her throat. There was more behind that suggestion than she wanted to contemplate.

"It's just an idea, m'm,"

Elizabeth took a deep breath. She needed to find someone, and soon. One had to do what one had to do. "And it's a good one, Polly. I shall notify the London Labour Exchange as soon as I get back. Meanwhile I'll see if Bessie can loan me one of her girls to help with the housework in time for the tour."

"That would be very nice, m'm. Thank you."

"Yes, well, here we are." Elizabeth walked into the low-roofed building that had once stabled the horses that pulled the carriages for the occupants of the manor house. There were no horses in the stables these days. They had all been sold to help pay Harry Compton's debts. Now there was nothing but a few bales of hay and some rusted and worn tackle hanging on the walls.

Doing her best to ignore the familiar melancholy she felt whenever entering the abandoned stables, Elizabeth made her way to the stall that housed her motorcycle. She stowed her handbag into the compartment behind the saddle, then grabbed the handles to wheel the machine out into the pale sunlight.

Thin clouds drifted across the sky, signaling rain on the way. Elizabeth hoped it would hold off until she returned home. Wet weather was a definite drawback to riding a motorcycle.

"Hop in," she told Polly, who was eyeing the narrow confines of the sidecar with doubt in her face.

"I've never ridden in a sidecar before, m'm."

"Oh, it's fun. You'll love it," Elizabeth assured her.

Looking entirely unconvinced, Polly hitched her skirt above her knees and climbed into the tiny compartment. Carefully she lowered herself onto the seat and tucked her legs into the space in front of her.

Elizabeth waited until she looked settled, then eased her leg over the saddle. "Hold tight," she said cheerfully, and slammed her foot down hard. The machine spluttered, then coughed, then let out a roar as it shuddered into life.

Polly let out a little squeal as Elizabeth gave it full throttle, and then they were away, bouncing over the rutted courtyard to the relatively smooth surface of the driveway.

As they swept down the hill, Elizabeth cast a glance at her passenger now and then, but the look of terror on Polly's face remained there until they came to a gentle stop in front of a row of cottages at the edge of the town.

Elizabeth silenced the roar of the engine and smiled at her secretary. "There. Nothing to it."

"Yes, m'm. Thank you, m'm." Polly heaved herself out of the sidecar and stood clutching her purse to her chest as if afraid she was about to lose it.

"You have the list I gave you?"

"Yes, m'm."

"It shouldn't take you too long to collect the rents. It largely depends on how many cups of tea you accept from the tenants."

"I could use a cup of tea right now." Polly gave a ghost of her usual grin. "Begging your pardon, m'm, but that was worse than riding in Sam's jeep. My legs feel like worn-out elastic, they do."

Elizabeth felt somewhat affronted. "You were perfectly safe, Polly. I'm very careful on the road."

"Oh, it weren't that, m'm," Polly said hastily. "It was just that I'd never ridden in a sidecar before, nor on a motorcycle, come to that. It takes some getting used to, I suppose."

"Yes, I suppose it does." Only slightly appeased, Elizabeth tucked the stray end of her scarf into her coat.

"I don't think I could ever ride a motorcycle on my own like you do," Polly said earnestly. "I think you ride it really, really well, m'm. That I do."

"Thank you, Polly." Reassured now, Elizabeth kick-started the engine again. "I'll pick you up at the crossroads about eleven o'clock." She rode off, forgetting all about Polly's frazzled nerves as she headed down the high street toward Bodkins the grocer's.

The queue outside the little shop stretched all the way around the corner when she got there. Parking her motorcycle across the street, she studied the straggly line of housewives with some trepidation.

It really wasn't fitting for the lady of the manor to queue up with the rest of the villagers to enter the shop. After all, it wasn't as if she were actually buying anything there. On the other hand, in these days of rationing

especially, it was tantamount to murder to walk past a
line of people to the head of the queue.

Elizabeth squared her shoulders. Whether they liked
it or not, she had a certain image to uphold, which she
had already compromised on more than one occasion.
Since she had spotted Rita Crumm in the queue, she
would not give that woman another opportunity to take
a stab at her with one of her well-aimed barbs.

Holding her head erect, Elizabeth strode across the
street and into the shop, only pausing long enough to
return several greetings from the queue with a regal
wave of her hand.

Percy Bodkins was behind the counter, looking ha-
rassed and out of sorts. His usual smile was missing
when he caught sight of her. In fact, he seemed even
more distressed to find the lady of the manor standing
in front of his counter. "Lady Elizabeth," he said, with
an obvious lack of enthusiasm. "This is a pleasant surprise. What can I do for you?"

Elizabeth cast an inquisitive eye over the contents of
the glass-fronted counter. "Good morning, Percy. I was
wondering if you had any of those little chocolate chips
that one puts in biscuits these days. Violet will be coming down for our weekly rations tomorrow and I know
she'd like to get some."

Percy looked blank. "Chocolate, your ladyship? All I
have is those little bars of chocolate over there. I don't
know anything about putting them in biscuits, though."

The little knot of customers in the shop had grown
amazingly quiet. Elizabeth raised her hand and pinched
two fingers together. "They're little round things. Chocolate chips, I think Bessie called them."

Percy shook his head, though he couldn't quite meet
her gaze. "Sorry, your ladyship. Haven't the faintest idea
what they are."

"Well, that's all right." She gave him a dazzling smile.
"What about peaches?"

"Peaches?"

"Peaches," Elizabeth repeated firmly.

"Sorry, m'm. No peaches."

"That's a pity, Percy."

"Yes, m'm. It is."

"I was rather hoping you'd know where I could get some."

"Sorry, your ladyship. Can't help you, I'm afraid."

Realizing that this conversation was going absolutely nowhere, Elizabeth gave up. Obviously, if she was going to get any information from Percy, she'd have to find a better place and a better way to do it. "Well, I shall just have to tell Violet to find something else to put in the biscuits."

Percy frowned. "Peaches in biscuits?"

"No, Percy. Chocolate chips. Are you quite sure you've never heard of them?"

Percy's gaze rested about two inches above her head. "Quite sure, your ladyship."

"Very well. Thank you, and good day to you, Percy." Elizabeth nodded and smiled at the women standing behind her, then made her way past them to the door. As she passed the window display, something caught her eye. She paused, frowning at a brace of chickens residing on a bed of green straw. The same kind of straw she'd spotted in the cricket pavilion.

Obviously Percy wasn't being completely honest with her. Something else was going on at the pavilion, other than a haven for lovers or private parties. And Percy Bodkins apparently knew more about it than he was willing to admit.

CHAPTER

8

Elizabeth continued on her way, wondering what she should do about her discovery. She didn't like it one bit. On the other hand, dealing in black market goods wasn't really hurting anyone, and could very well benefit the villagers who had been sorely deprived of wholesome food.

She had been known to bend the rules a little herself in order to help out the less privileged. Maybe she should simply let it lie. It was doubtful that either Sid or George, being little more than reluctant remnants of Sitting Marsh's local constabulary, would notice that the villagers were eating a bit better nowadays. Even if they did detect an excess of formerly unobtainable edibles floating around town, it was unlikely they would do anything about it.

Still absorbed in the problem, Elizabeth almost missed the elderly lady emerging from the post office across the street. By the time she recognized Henrietta Jones, the old woman was hobbling off at a surprising speed down the road.

Without thinking, Elizabeth called out after her, intending to invite her to share a pot of tea in Bessie's bakeshop. Henrietta, of course, failed to hear her, and Elizabeth watched her turn the corner and disappear. Someone, it seemed, had been kind enough to give Henrietta a lift into town. Perhaps she needn't have worried about her after all.

Polly seemed a little more cheerful on the way back, and even managed to carry on a shouted conversation as they rode sedately up the hill to the Manor House.

Everyone had paid their rents, much to Elizabeth's relief. She hated having to remind her tenants they owed money. It didn't happen very often, but when it did, she felt embarrassed by the fact that she needed the money every bit as much as they did. Since she had turned over more of the accounting to Polly, she had impressed upon the girl the need to keep her financial position a secret from everyone.

The villagers looked up to the lady of the manor, relying on her to take care of them in times of crisis, to offer them advice and solutions to their problems, and to protect their homes and their way of life. If they knew that she was struggling to keep the Manor House solvent in the face of mounting debts, they would lose confidence in her. She would lose their respect.

Since she had a tradition to uphold, established by a long line of noble ancestors, and in view of the fact that she was the first woman to hold such a position, she would go to great lengths to keep her unfortunate and, with any luck temporary, lack of funds a secret. Therefore Polly was on notice that should the news leak out, she would be immediately dismissed.

Major Monroe was the only outsider who knew about

her state of affairs, and she could trust him implicitly to be discreet.

Thinking of Earl, she wondered what he thought about his squadron leader's arrest. She was rather anxious to talk to him about that, but the meeting would have to wait for now. First she had to deal with the American investigators, and she wasn't looking forward to it at all.

When the two men were ushered into the library that afternoon by a disapproving Martin, Elizabeth was instantly reminded of the American movies she'd seen about the FBI.

Both men wore trilbies, which Elizabeth had recently learned were called fedoras by the Americans. They also wore raincoats over their uniforms, belted at the waist. She had never been able to understand why American men tied their belts instead of buckling them. Then again, she was beginning to realize there were many more differences between the two nations than she'd ever suspected, including the language.

She greeted the two investigators with her usual graceful charm, but unlike the American officers she'd previously encountered, these two looked particularly unimpressed.

"We'd like to talk to your secretary," the taller one said, after introducing himself as Captain Johansen.

"I've sent for her," Elizabeth said, somewhat haughtily. She was determined to keep up appearances, no matter what. "Please take a seat. Can I have Martin take your coats?"

"No, ma'am. If you don't mind. It's a little chilly in here." The captain nodded at his companion. "This is Lieutenant Wiles."

Elizabeth smiled at the other man. He had sandy hair, and clutched his hat as if he were afraid she was going to steal it. His eyes were very blue, and very cold. Not at all like Earl's, which were also steel blue, but unlike the lieutenant, his were usually as warm and pleasing as the early summer sky.

Lieutenant Wiles failed to return her smile and she walked over to the fireplace, trying to regain her confidence, which wasn't often shaken. She wished Earl could have been there with her to give her support. These men intimidated her for some reason. It wasn't a feeling she was accustomed to, and it unsettled her considerably.

In an effort to keep things on a sociable level, she turned to face them. "May I offer you some hot tea?"

Captain Johansen relaxed his features a fraction. "Coffee would be nice, ma'am, if you have some."

"I'm sure we can manage to find some somewhere." She rang the bell that would summon Martin. Eventually. When a polite tap on the door came almost immediately, she was taken aback for a moment, until instead of her butler, Polly slipped into the room, her face as white as chalk. Her dark eyes looked huge as she shot a frightened glance at the two men, then stared at Elizabeth in mute appeal.

"Come over here, Polly." Elizabeth held out her hand. "Gentlemen, this is Polly Barnett, my assistant. Polly, this is Captain Johansen and Lieutenant Wiles."

"How do you do, sir," Polly said weakly.

Both men touched their foreheads. "Ma'am," they said in unison.

"Sit down, Polly," Elizabeth said firmly. "I'm sure these gentlemen won't take too long."

"We just have a question or two to ask." The captain pulled a notebook from inside his raincoat.

Since both men remained standing, Elizabeth sat down herself before saying pointedly, "I think it would make these proceedings more relaxing if you both took a seat."

"Thank you, ma'am." Captain Johansen sat down on the very edge of a deep, velvet-covered armchair, while the lieutenant chose the window seat. Neither man looked very comfortable, which made Elizabeth feel slightly better.

Martin must not have been too far away. Just as the captain began to speak, a tap on the door interrupted him. The butler shuffled into the room, peering over the top of his gold-rimmed glasses. "You rang, madam?"

"Yes, Martin. Would you ask Violet to send up some coffee and biscuits. Perhaps some of that cake she made last night?"

"Yes, madam." Martin turned to leave, just as Captain Johansen asked Polly, "At what time did you see Squadron Leader Cutter on the night Private Morris was murdered?"

Polly swallowed a couple of times, and sent a hunted look in Elizabeth's direction.

"Just tell them the truth," Elizabeth said quietly. "You have nothing to be afraid of, Polly."

"Yes, m'm." Polly looked down at her hands and twisted them together in her lap. "I saw him when we got to the church. He was with the other officers and he told me he'd just got there a few minutes before I did. That was a long time after the bells had stopped ringing. Me mum and me sister and me had to stop and get dressed before we went down there."

"And when was the last time you saw him before that?"

Again Polly hesitated, then said in a small voice, "At the Tudor Arms on Saturday night."

"When he was fighting with Private Morris?"

Polly looked as if she were about to cry. "Yes, but—"

"You didn't see him again until you saw him at the church on Sunday night?"

"No, sir, I didn't."

"Excuse me, madam," Martin said from the doorway. "I remember the church bells ringing that night."

"Yes, Martin, I'm sure you do." Elizabeth smiled

apologetically at the captain. "Martin was quite upset. The bells woke us all up—"

"No, madam. I beg your pardon, but I was already awake. It was the young American who had woken me up. The wind must have caught the door as he left. It slammed very hard indeed. It was quite some time after that when the bells rang."

The captain gave him a sharp look. "Young American? Are you talking about Squadron Leader Sam Cutter?"

Martin appeared offended at being spoken to so harshly. "I believe that is the gentleman's name, yes."

"Do you know what time he left the house?"

Elizabeth cut in. "Martin sometimes gets confused, Captain. I'm sure he doesn't remember what time it was."

"Oh, but I do, madam. I remember precisely. I heard the grandfather clock in the hall chime twice as I stood at the window."

Elizabeth's gasp of dismay sounded loud in the quiet room.

The captain looked down at his notes. "According to the squadron leader, he attended a card game on the base, then returned home shortly before midnight. Did anyone see him enter the house?"

"Why don't you ask his fellow officers?" Elizabeth suggested. "They must know what time he arrived home."

"They do." Captain Johansen lifted his head. "They confirmed he arrived at the time he said he did. It's the time he left again that we can't agree on. No one remembers seeing him in the room when the church bells rang, and now, if this gentleman is correct—"

"There is no question about it," Martin declared, sounding more lucid than he had in weeks. "I heard a noise and went to my window to investigate. I saw the American chap running down the steps and across the courtyard. The moon was very bright that night. I saw his face quite clearly."

Of course Martin had to choose this time to experience a clear mind, Elizabeth thought. "Thank you, Martin," she said quickly. "The coffee, please?"

"Yes, madam." With a courtly little bow, Martin left the room.

"Sam did leave before the bells rang," Polly said suddenly. "He was at my house."

Elizabeth threw her a startled glance. Heavens, surely the child was not going to lie in order to save the squadron leader?

The captain pounced on her at once. "Didn't you tell me you didn't see Cutter that night until you arrived at the church?"

Polly stared steadily into the man's suspicious face. "Yes, I did. That *was* when I first saw him. Sam and I'd had a row, and he came to my house that night to make up. It was late and everyone was asleep. He told me he sat outside my house for a long time trying to think what he wanted to say, and wondering whether he should wake me up or not. Then he heard the bells ringing and everyone started coming out of their houses. Sam said he didn't want to get me in trouble, so he drove back past the church and that's when he saw his mates, so he went over to join them."

The captain made no comment, but just sat there scribbling in his notebook. Elizabeth glanced at Lieutenant Wiles and tried to read his expression. Neither man was giving much away.

"So you see," Polly said, a little desperately, "it couldn't have been Sam that murdered Kenny Morris. He didn't go near the church until after the bells stopped ringing and everyone saw him there with his mates. If he'd done the murder, he wouldn't have hung around like that, would he?"

"Who knows what a guy will do when he's under

stress," Captain Johansen murmured. "Or what he'll say. My guess is that he met Morris at the church, they fought, cutting Cutter's hand in the struggle. Cutter choked Morris with the bell rope, making the bells ring, then panicked. He was on his way to your house, perhaps to hide, or at least ask for help, when he saw everyone heading for the church. He turned around and headed back. When he saw his fellow officers, he joined them, hoping they'd cover for him. Luckily for them, they didn't."

Polly, who had been shaking her head throughout this dispassionate speech, burst out, "No! He didn't do it. I know he didn't do it. He cut his hand on a broken bottle at the card game. He told me that's what happened." She was obviously doing her best not to cry, and Elizabeth put an arm around her shoulders.

"It's all right, Polly," she murmured, knowing in her heart that it wasn't all right at all. Turning back to the captain, she asked quietly, "Would it be possible for me to have a word with the squadron leader?"

Polly immediately looked hopeful.

The captain, however, shook his head. "Sorry, ma'am. Cutter is confined to barracks. He's not talking to anyone right now."

Polly sniffed, and hunted for her handkerchief.

A light tap on the door broke the awkward silence that followed. Martin appeared, carrying a tray with a silver coffeepot and several small cups and saucers.

Elizabeth nudged Polly, who jumped up and took the tray from the elderly man's shaking hands.

She managed a timid smile, and Martin peered at her over the top of his glasses. "Are you all right, miss?"

She looked surprised, but gave him a quick nod. "Thank you, Martin." She put the tray down on the low table in front of Elizabeth. "Shall I pour, your ladyship?"

Elizabeth gave her a smile of approval. Things were looking up. Not so long ago Polly would have dumped the tray down and fled the room. "That would be very nice, Polly. Thank you."

"Will that be all, madam?" Martin inquired.

"Yes, thank you, Martin."

"Very well, madam."

He left the room again, and Elizabeth noticed with a flash of amusement that both the lieutenant and the captain stared after him with a faint air of disbelief. No doubt this was their first encounter with a genuine English butler. They probably didn't know what to make of him.

She watched Polly carefully pour the coffee into each demitasse. After handing Elizabeth the tiny cup and saucer, she served the same to each of the Americans, both of whom accepted them as if they'd never seen coffee before.

"Cream, your ladyship?" Polly, who was obviously doing her best to impress, poured a small amount of cream from the silver jug, then turned to the captain.

He shook his head. "I'll take it black, thanks."

"Our coffee is a little stronger than you're accustomed to," Elizabeth said, remembering the first time Earl had tasted the English version. "You might want to add a little cream."

The lieutenant was already lifting the cup to his lips, which looked even smaller in his pudgy hand.

Both Elizabeth and Polly watched with interest as he took a hearty sip. An instant later his face screwed up as if he'd bitten into a lemon. For a moment Elizabeth thought he would spit out the bitter brew, but with remarkable presence of mind he swallowed it down, albeit with a shudder. Pretty much the same reaction Earl had had. He'd learned to take cream with his coffee after that.

Apparently deciding that he wasn't going to risk it, Captain Johansen put his cup down untouched. "We must be getting back to the base, ma'am. Thank you for your time."

"Not at all." Elizabeth rose, and both men jumped to their feet. "I'm sorry we can't help you any further."

"Oh, I think you've helped a great deal." The captain touched his forehead with his fingers. "We'll see ourselves out, ma'am."

She inclined her head in graceful acknowledgment.

Pulling his hat on his head, the captain walked briskly to the door, followed by the lieutenant.

Polly waited until the door had closed behind them before saying glumly, "He's bloomin' right. We helped him all right. We helped make things worse for Sam, didn't we?"

"You told the truth, Polly, that's all that matters."

"I wish he would have let you talk to Sam, m'm. I know you would have found a way to help him. You're so good at that."

Elizabeth frowned. "I wish I could have had a word with him. Maybe Major Monroe can help. I'll talk to him about it."

"Oh, would you, m'm?"

Elizabeth hated to raise false hopes in the child, but she didn't have the heart to disappoint her right then. Polly had been through enough for one day. "I don't know what he can do to help," she said, trying to sound positive, "but I'm sure he'll come up with something."

The truth was, she was anxious to talk to Earl and find out exactly what his opinions were about Sam Cutter. From everything she'd heard, the young man could be in serious trouble. He had a motive, means, and opportunity. And only his word for an alibi.

There was also no proof, however, that he hadn't been telling Polly the truth about the way he cut his hand and that he'd sat outside her house while Kenny was fighting for his life in the bell tower. Perhaps a word with his fellow officers might help. She made up her mind to ask Earl about it that very evening.

As it happened, Earl arrived back from the base earlier than usual that day. All operations had been suspended, thanks to an approaching storm over the channel, he told her, when he surprised her on the back terrace as she was attempting to teach the puppies to come to her on command.

"Perhaps you'd care to join me for dinner tonight?" she suggested, hoping passionately that Violet had something suitable in the larder.

"Sounds great." He smiled at her, though knowing him as well as she did, she detected a deep concern behind the warmth in his light blue eyes.

How she longed to smooth away those worry lines in his forehead. The ache in her heart almost took her breath away. She heard herself saying, "How about an aperitif in the conservatory beforehand? About seven?" Just the thought of being alone with him in her special place made her heart beat faster. It was wrong, and it was forbidden—this secret yearning she felt for him. And so utterly inescapable.

From the moment she had first set eyes on the handsome major, she had been unable to control this fluttering inside whenever she was near him. Fortunately for her, Earl was married, and therefore unobtainable. For had it been otherwise, she might have foolishly compromised her heart, and that was something she had sworn never to do again.

Yet, there were times, like right now, watching his fingers ruffle the soft fur at Gracie's neck, a smile lurking at his mouth, when the ache became almost unbearable.

He looked up, and caught her watching him. His face stilled, and for an eternal moment it was as if she were captured by the sudden knowledge in his eyes, then he dropped his chin and scooped up the wriggling mass of black and white fur.

"They're growing fast," he said, heaving Gracie up above his head. "Getting heavy, too."

Fool! She was such a fool. Had she given away her feelings in her expression? She sincerely hoped not. She didn't want anything to spoil this fragile friendship she had with the major. If he knew how she really felt about him, she was quite certain he would feel honor bound to withdraw, and she would lose what had become a treasured part of her life.

Still trembling inside from the impact of that pregnant moment, she managed a light laugh. "They are, indeed. It won't be long before they have outgrown their space in the scullery. I'll have to find them a bigger room. They have a preference for the drawing room, or the library whenever they can escape Violet's clutches, but I'm afraid Martin would never tolerate having them underfoot all the time."

"What about the stables? They'd have plenty of room there. At the rate they're growing, they'll need more room than you can give them in the house."

"Oh, I hate to put them out there. It gets so cold in the stables in the winter."

Earl laughed. "Their coats will keep them warm. They're outside dogs, Elizabeth. They need to roam. Give them a home in the stables, somewhere sheltered and dry to sleep, plenty of food and water, and they'll be perfectly happy to patrol your land for you. They'll make great watchdogs."

She wrinkled her brow. "You don't think they'll wander off and get lost?"

"Not if they know there's a bowl of chow waiting for them when they get back."

"I suppose you're right."

She must have communicated her doubts, as he sat back on his heels and studied her face. "If it will make you feel any better, I'll build a fence for them so they can't get out unless someone is with them. At least until they get used to their freedom. If it's cold, you can always bring them into the house at night to sleep."

She let out a sigh. "All right, I'll try it. But at the very first sign that they are unhappy out there, I'm bringing them right back into the house."

He grinned at her, warming her as no roaring fire ever could. "Attagirl! Give me a few days to get the fence up, and we'll move George and Gracie into their new home."

She forgot about her concerns over Polly and Sam Cutter. She forgot about Percy's illicit dealings in black market goods. She forgot that the chimneys needed to be swept and a host of strangers would be invading the Manor House at the weekend. All she could think about right then was the way the breeze ruffled Earl Monroe's hair, and how intensely she longed to smooth it back with her fingers.

CHAPTER

❧ 9 ❧

In the end Elizabeth decided to wait until the evening before tackling Earl on the subject of Sam's arrest. She dressed with care for her engagement with him, in a dress of soft rose wool that had always been one of her favorites. She even allowed her hair to settle on her shoulders, instead of secured in a twist as she normally wore it.

Martin spied her on her way to the conservatory and raised his eyebrows. "I hardly recognized you, madam. For a moment I thought it was Lady Wellsborough walking down the hallway toward me. Gave me quite a start."

Elizabeth smiled. "Why, thank you, Martin. How very gallant of you. That is quite a compliment."

Martin cleared his throat. "Quite. Violet informs me you will be dining in the banquet room tonight, with a guest."

"Yes, I have invited Major Monroe for dinner this

evening. He has been very generous of late with his gifts of wine and spirits, not to mention, I suspect, other items for Violet's larder. I thought it time we repaid him."

Why on earth, she wondered, was she defending herself to Martin? It was none of his business why she had invited Earl to dinner. There was absolutely no need for her to be making excuses.

"I see, madam." Martin's eyelid dropped in what suspiciously resembled a wink. "I'm sure it will be a pleasurable experience."

"Yes, well," Elizabeth said lightly, "one has to do what one can under the circumstances."

"Precisely, madam." He shuffled off, leaving her with the uncomfortable feeling that she was the only one in the household who believed her unfortunate fascination with the major was a secret.

Unsettled by the notion, she was somewhat restrained with her greeting when Violet showed Earl into the conservatory that evening. Her housekeeper's frown of disapproval did nothing to ease her discomfort. She waited until Earl was seated with a glass of sherry in his hand before saying what had been on her mind all afternoon.

"Do you think Sam Cutter is guilty of murder?"

His answer was swift and decisive. "Hell, no." He shot her an apologetic glance. "Excuse me, Elizabeth. It's just that holding Sam for that murder is such a load of bunk. I know my men, and Sam would no more strangle a guy than I would."

"I'm sorry, Earl. It must be awful for you to have someone in your charge suspected of such a horrible crime."

"The tough part is not being able to do much about it. I don't suppose you've heard anything that might help?"

"I'm sorry, not a thing." Because she'd been far too busy worrying about Percy and his black market goods, she thought with a pang of guilt.

"Ah, well, I've been ordered to stay out of the investigation in any case."

Elizabeth stared at him in surprise. "Really? Why?"

Earl shrugged. "Those blockheads Johansen and Wiles didn't want my help. More or less told me I was interfering in business that didn't concern me. What the heck do they know about Sam Cutter? They've got the wrong man, and they're too darn bullheaded to see it."

"They have no real proof that Sam killed Kenny Morris, do they?"

"I don't know what they've got. Circumstantial, I guess. Enough to hold him confined to barracks, anyway."

"It's really unfortunate he fought with Kenny at the Tudor Arms, then again at the card game. That doesn't help his case, I'm afraid."

"Don't I know it." Earl gazed gloomily into his glass. "Except he wasn't the only one involved in the fight at that card game."

"Perhaps, but he was the only one with a grudge against Kenny Morris, wasn't he?"

Earl's dark gaze flicked up at her. "Sounds as if you agree with the investigators. Do you know something I don't?"

She shook her head, smiling to dispel his concern. "I'm simply trying to see things from every angle, that's all."

He took a sip from his glass. "Well, as a matter of fact, there was someone else there that night who had a beef against Kenny. Some civilian who Kenny had smuggled onto the base for the card game. I guess the guy had come down from London for the weekend. Anyway, both Sam and Kenny lost a bundle of cash to this guy, and Morris accused him of cheating. That's what started the fight."

Elizabeth sat up straight. "Really? The investigators didn't mention him this afternoon."

Earl grunted. "You don't expect them to tell you anything, do you? They wouldn't even talk to me. In fact, I had to sneak in to talk to Sam, which is how I found out about this Forrester guy."

Elizabeth blinked. "Forrester? *Brian* Forrester?"

It was Earl's turn to look surprised. "Yeah, you know him?"

"Well, I think I do. If it's the same Brian Forrester—and I can't imagine there being two men with that name from London—then he's accompanying a group of elderly citizens on a tour of the Manor House this Saturday."

Earl smiled. "Small world, isn't it?"

Worried, Elizabeth said nervously, "Do you think he might have strangled Kenny Morris?"

Earl shrugged. "Who knows. From what I've heard, there were more than a few people gunning for Kenny. I'm surprised he made it this long without a knife being stuck in him in some dark alley. Not too popular, our Kenny."

"So I gather."

"Anyway, Sam swears he saw a car close by the church the night Kenny was murdered. He thought it might be one of his guys . . . er . . . you know, smooching in the backseat with one of the locals."

Elizabeth nodded, and tried to resist the image of herself snuggling in the backseat of a car with Earl.

"Well, apparently the car was empty. No one in it. Sam thought that was kind of strange, leaving a car on the side of the road like that."

"Very few people actually own a car in Sitting Marsh." She frowned. "What kind of car was it?"

"He wasn't familiar with the model and didn't think to look, but he says it was a black sedan."

Elizabeth's mind flashed back a couple of days, to when she stood at the window, watching a black sedan pull away down her driveway. "Oh, my. Brian Forrester drives a black sedan."

Earl's gaze sharpened. "Is that right? Well, we've got his address. As a matter of fact, an officer is on his way to London right now to talk to this Forrester. Maybe something will come of it, maybe not. Right now, I'd say Sam is in a pretty tight spot."

"What about the knife? Do they know to whom it belonged?"

Earl sighed. "It was Kenny's knife. Several guys said they saw him with it, and it had his initials on it. Looks like he tried to use it on whoever killed him, and they turned the tables on him."

"Then surely it was self-defense."

"Maybe. I guess it depends on the reason someone was meeting Kenny that late at night in a churchyard."

"Kenny Morris could have lured Brian Forrester there to get his money back."

"It's possible, I guess. We'll just have to wait and see what the investigating officer has to say when he gets back from London."

If Brian Forrester was guilty of murder, Elizabeth thought ruefully, there would be no tour of her home on Saturday. She wasn't sure how she felt about that. One thing was certain: Polly would be ecstatic.

"So tell me about the cricket match," Earl said, mercifully putting an end to what had become a harrowing conversation. "What's the latest on that?"

Eager to cast her mind onto a more pleasant subject, Elizabeth said brightly, "Well, Polly contacted the army camp in Beerstowe. The commanding officer there was quite accommodating, and promised us a cricket team for next week. He seemed quite eager to take up the challenge. What about your chaps?"

Earl nodded. "Got about a dozen guys all raring to go. Though I don't think any one of them knows a darn thing about cricket."

"Well, I think we can help out there. A few of the villagers have volunteered to teach your team the rudiments of the game. I'm not sure how much they can teach you in one evening, but if you could have your men on the cricket field as early as possible on Monday evening, they can certainly do their best to give them an idea of what it's all about."

Earl rubbed his chin. "I guess we can manage that. I'll check it out when I get back and let you know. What about the game itself?"

"Well, we've set it for next Wednesday afternoon. Two o'clock. Can you manage that?"

"I guess so. We'll put it down for then, but remember there are no guarantees that we can make it. This is wartime, after all."

"I understand. If it doesn't work out, I suppose we can postpone it, and perhaps your men will be back in time to help us finish up the food, instead." Since they probably provided much of it in the first place, she reflected.

"Well, let's hope we'll be able to give the Jerries a break next week." Earl looked up as Martin knocked discreetly on the door and opened it.

"Dinner is served, madam," he announced.

Elizabeth stood, and smiled at her guest. "Come, let's see what magic Violet has managed to conjure up from our rations tonight."

He grinned and rose to his feet. "Lead the way. I'm beginning to like this English food, even if you guys have never heard of spices and herbs."

"We've heard of them," Elizabeth said, remembering Violet's peppery dish the night before. "We've just never learned how to use them. I hate to admit it, but when it comes to cooking, the French definitely have the upper hand."

She led the way to the dining room, certain of one thing. No matter what Martin brought to the table that night, the very fact that Earl was there to share it with her would make it a feast for the gods. Right now, she couldn't ask for anything more.

The following morning the entire household staff was put to the task of cleaning the chimneys. Desmond arrived on the kitchen doorstep, weighed down by the long-handled circular brushes and extensions. Violet and Polly had already covered the furniture in all the main rooms with sheets and blankets—most of which had been pulled from the beds and would have to be replaced by nightfall.

The fireplaces in the empty bedrooms had been blocked by sheets of newspaper. Those chimneys would have to wait until another time to be cleaned. Polly had waited until everyone had left the officers' quarters in the east wing, then scurried around to get everything covered up before the major operation began.

Finally, they were all ready. Assembled in the library, Elizabeth, Polly, and Violet stood by as Desmond approached the first chimney.

Martin had been stationed outside to signal when he saw the brush appear through the chimney on the roof. Violet stood close enough to the window to see him, while Polly and Elizabeth were poised to help Desmond with whatever he needed.

"All right, your ladyship," Desmond announced, sounding a lot less confident now that he was actually faced with the daunting project. "I think we're ready."

Looking at his frail, bowed shoulders, Elizabeth wondered for the first time if the old man had the strength to push those wicked-looking brushes all the way up the chimney. Maybe she should have asked around the village for someone to take on the task after all. It would have meant paying them, of course, but remembering some of her disastrous attempts at managing her own repairs, she was uncomfortably reminded that sometimes it cost her more money in the long run.

"Now, your ladyship," Desmond announced, his voice muffled as he stuck his head inside the fireplace, "all I have to do is shove this here brush all the way up to the top and then pull it down again, giving it a twist or two on the way down."

"Very well." Elizabeth smiled at Polly to reassure her. "Polly and I will be here should you need help." Thought what help they could be, she hadn't the faintest idea.

"Thank you, m'm." Desmond heaved the brush into the fireplace and began nudging it up the chimney, while Elizabeth watched in concern as thick black flakes of soot began to fall. The long handle gradually disappeared, and Desmond paused to screw in the extension. "Shouldn't be long now, m'm," he said, a little breathlessly.

"Good show." Elizabeth looked at Violet, whose expression suggested that at any minute total disaster was about to strike. "Keep an eye on Martin, Violet," she said, giving her an encouraging nod. "Let us know the second he signals."

Violet glanced out of the window. "I don't know how the old fool's going to see anything with his glasses perched on top of his head. In any case, he's looking at the wrong chimney."

Elizabeth sighed. "Maybe you should go down there with him. Polly can stand by the window. Desmond appears to be managing quite well by himself."

Violet huffed her annoyance, but hurried out of the room.

"I don't know as that is strictly true, m'm," Desmond said, his voice barely intelligible. He went on grunting and pushing, and Elizabeth peered into the fireplace at him.

"What isn't strictly true, Desmond?"

"That I'm managing by meself."

More grunting and pushing ensued, while Polly muttered, "Oh, crikey."

"Is there a problem, Desmond?" Elizabeth crossed her fingers and tried not to hear Violet's voice saying, *I told you so*.

"Just a slight one, your ladyship. I do believe I could use a little of that help you were talking about, so to speak."

Polly groaned.

Elizabeth eyed the black flakes snowing down on Desmond's back. Reluctantly, she asked, "What can we do to help?"

Desmond grunted again, and eased himself out of the fireplace. Polly gasped. Elizabeth could hardly blame her. Desmond looked as if he were taking part in a minstrel show. The peak of his cap was thick with soot, and his pale eyes seemed to glow eerily in his grimy face. "It's stuck, m'm," he said with a note of defeat. "Can't budge it at all."

"Oh, dear." Elizabeth glanced at Polly, who glared at Desmond as if she'd like to throttle him. "Well, I suppose we'll have to help. Maybe if all three of us pull on it?"

Polly gave her a look of desperation. "What, with me best jumper on and all?"

Elizabeth wasn't too keen on wading into that filthy fireplace wearing one of her good silk blouses, either, but right then she could see no alternative. "It's all for a good cause," she told Polly. "Try to remember that."

"Can't we wear something over our clothes, m'm?"

Elizabeth thought for a moment. "I think Violet has some of my father's old nightshirts tucked away in the oak chest. I'll see if I can find them. Polly, you go down to the hall stand and collect some scarves and gloves. That old felt farmer's hat will help, and I think there's a beret down there."

Polly rushed from the room, and Elizabeth bent over to look at Desmond, who was still crouched in the fireplace. "We'll be back in a tick," she told him. "Meanwhile, do your best to get the dratted thing loose, there's a good man."

"I'll do what I can, your ladyship."

Obviously he didn't have much hope of success in that quarter, judging by the tone in his voice. Hoping for the best anyway, Elizabeth hurried up to the east wing, where the oak chest was stored.

Several minutes later she returned to the library with the nightshirts. Polly was already there, a beret crammed on her head to protect her hair. Desmond was still tugging fruitlessly on the handle of the brush, dislodging more soot with every grunt.

Elizabeth handed Polly one of the long red flannel gowns, and pulled the other one over her head. Polly had brought the soft felt farmer's hat and Elizabeth pulled it down over her hair, then tugged on the gloves Polly gave her. Feeling somewhat like an overstuffed scarecrow, she smiled at her grim-looking secretary. "Ready?"

Polly squared her shoulders. "Yes, mum."

Beginning to enjoy the little adventure, Elizabeth said heartily, "Then to battle!"

She edged into the fireplace and grasped the handle of the brush just above Desmond's grimy hands. Polly squeezed in beside her and grabbed hold of the remaining visible part of the handle.

"Thank heavens this fireplace was built several centuries ago," Elizabeth said, her voice echoing up the chimney. "If this had been a modern fireplace, we wouldn't have managed to get Desmond in here, much less all three of us."

"If I may suggest, m'm," Desmond said, "on the count of three we all pull together."

"Good idea," Elizabeth took a firm grip on the brush. "You count off, Desmond."

"Right, m'm. Are we ready, then? One, two, *three!*"

The last word squeezed out of his lungs as he put his weight on the handle. Elizabeth tugged and tugged, while Polly made a straining sound in her throat.

Soot fell thicker, and Polly spat, then hastily apologized. "Sorry, m'm."

Elizabeth had no breath to answer her. She was afraid to breathe in, and the effort of holding the air in her lungs while hauling on the handle was making her head spin.

Then the handle gave a little shudder and a jerk. "It's coming, m'm," Desmond panted and then, all at once, indeed it came—in a swirling, choking, blinding cascade of soot.

Polly shrieked and leaped out of the fireplace, sending Elizabeth sprawling. She couldn't see, and tugged off her gloves to wipe the black dust out of her eyes.

Struggling to sit up, she heard an all too familiar voice. "Excuse me, Lady Elizabeth? I couldn't find anyone so I . . . What the—? Are you okay?"

Miserably she looked up into the concerned face of Earl Monroe.

For a long moment he stared at her in disbelief, then, much to her mortification, he threw back his head with an unrestrained roar of laughter.

She sat there, face grimed with soot, an old felt hat dragged over her hair, shapeless red flannel gown bundled up around her knees, and felt like howling.

"We made a bit of a mess, m'm," Polly said unnecessarily.

Elizabeth tightened her mouth and glared at Earl. "Don't stand there giggling at me, you idiot. Help me up. Please."

Earl stopped laughing and held out his hand. "Sorry, your ladyship."

Elizabeth grabbed on tight, and with what little dignity she had left, scrambled to her feet. "There, that wasn't so bad, was it? At least we got the brush out."

Earl studied the fireplace, where Desmond was unscrewing the extension on the brush. "Good thing you moved the rugs out of the way." He looked back at her feet. "I suggest you not walk across them in those shoes, though."

The door flew open just then and Violet marched in. "Polly! Why weren't you watching out the window? There I am, jumping up and down like a jack-in-the-box and you're . . . not . . . there . . ." Her voice gradually trailed off as she surveyed the three would-be chimney sweeps. "Goodness gracious me! What in the world happened?"

"We were sweeping the chimney," Elizabeth said calmly. "One's bound to get a little grubby, Violet. It's only to be expected."

For once Violet had no answer. In fact, right then the only sound in the room was Earl's raucous laughter.

CHAPTER

❈ 10 ❈

Violet, in her usual bossy way, quickly took command of the situation. In no time at all she had the filthy nightshirts bundled up under her arm, ordered Polly to collect the hats, gloves, and shoes, and marched along the hall with her to the laundry chute.

Desmond, after removing his own shoes, announced that he could manage the rest of the chimneys on his own. "I know what I was doing wrong now, your ladyship. Wrong size brush, that was it. Now that I know what I'm doing, I think I'll manage it all better on me own."

"Well, Elizabeth said doubtfully, "if you're sure."

"I'm positive, m'm. Don't you worry." He trudged out of the room, the blackened brush under his arm.

Elizabeth looked around the library and sighed. "Now I'll have to get help for Polly. She'll never get all this cleaned up by the weekend." Aware that Earl was watching her with amusement still brimming in his eyes, she self-consciously wiped her forehead with the back of her hand. "I'd better get this mess cleaned off my face."

Earl tilted his head and regarded her with a quizzical expression. "Oh, I don't know. Kind of suits you."

She made a face at him, but before she could come back with a retort, the telephone jangled on her office desk. She waited a moment or two to see if someone would pick it up, but when it continued to ring, she said with a sigh, "I'd better answer that."

He nodded. "I've gotta run, anyway."

It wasn't until after he'd left the room that she remembered he hadn't said why he'd been looking for her in the library.

The voice that answered her breathless greeting on the telephone was something of a shock. "Just wanted to confirm things with you, Lady Elizabeth," Brian Forrester announced. "I'm estimating our time of arrival on Saturday at roughly one o'clock. Shouldn't take more than a couple of hours to tour the Manor House, do you think?"

Taken off guard, Elizabeth took a moment to compose her thoughts. "That sounds about right, Mr. Forrester." She hesitated for a moment. "By the way, a gentleman was asking for you. I think he was an officer from the American base here in Sitting Marsh. Did he get in touch with you?"

Her heart skipped a nervous beat when the pause went on too long, then Forrester said carefully, "As a matter of fact, your ladyship, he just left. Asked me a lot of questions about the night that Yank was murdered. Unfortunately, I was unable to help him. Didn't see a thing."

"I see." Disappointed, Elizabeth realized she'd been hoping that Forrester would be arrested, thereby clearing Sam Cutter of suspicion. Since it appeared that Forrester wasn't a suspect after all, prospects did not seem too optimistic for Polly's boyfriend.

Elizabeth could not shake the niggling guilt that maybe she wasn't doing enough to find out what happened that night in the bell tower. She had more or less promised Earl she would ask questions in the village, and she'd been far too lax about it.

Immediately after lunch she rode her motorcycle into town, determined to make amends for her lack of effort in the investigation. Although Earl hadn't said anything, now that he was officially ordered off the case, she was the only chance he had left to help clear Sam Cutter. That's if the young officer really was innocent.

Both Polly and Earl had seemed convinced that the young man hadn't killed Kenny Morris, but she had only their word to go on. She needed more information, and there was only one way to get it.

She spent most of the afternoon talking to various people in the village, most of whom had never met Sam Cutter or Kenny Morris. When she stopped by the hairdresser's shop, however, she had better luck.

Marlene Barnett, Polly's sister, was eager to talk to her. Leaving her customer seated under the hair dryer, she gave Elizabeth her version of the fight in the Tudor Arms.

"If Sam hadn't been there that night, Lady Elizabeth," Marlene declared, "I don't know what would have happened to Polly. That Kenny Morris was scaring us both, that I do know. Sam took care of him, though." She caught her breath, then hurried on, "Oh, I didn't mean he killed him or nothing like that, your ladyship. Sam would never be that mean. Our Polly knows him really well, and she wouldn't go with no one that was mean."

"Did you happen to see Sam the night of the murder?" Elizabeth asked her. "Before you saw him at the church, that is."

Marlene shook her head. "No, m'm. The first time I saw Sam was when we all went down there. He was with the rest of the Yanks. I did see Kenny Morris, though. I was letting the cat out before I went to bed that night and I heard a jeep coming down the road. It was Kenny. The moon was really bright that night and he passed right by me. He must have been on his way to the church."

Elizabeth narrowed her eyes. "Do you know what time that was?"

"Not exactly." Marlene glanced at the clock on the wall. "Must have been around two o'clock, though. I was up late that night, reading my library book. I fell asleep in the armchair. I must have been really tired. I don't usually do that. Anyway, I woke up and the fire had died down. I noticed the time then, it was a quarter to two. I made meself some Ovaltine and then put the cat out. Couldn't have been more than ten or fifteen minutes."

"And Sam's jeep wasn't outside the house when Kenny went by?"

"No, m'm. I would have seen him sitting there."

"What did you do after you let the cat out?"

"Went to bed, m'm, didn't I. Not that it did much good. An hour later we was all up chasing down to the church, scared to death there was an invasion."

"And you didn't hear the jeep come back again?"

Marlene frowned. "Well, I thought I heard it, but I was half asleep at the time, so I can't be sure."

"Well, thank you for your help, Marlene." Elizabeth glanced at the row of women seated under the hair dryers, all of whom, she suspected, were pretending to read their magazines while straining their ears to overhear her conversation with the hairdresser. "If you should hear anything at all about that night that you think might be of interest, please ring me at the Manor House."

Marlene nodded. "I'd tell Polly, in any case. She could pass it on."

"Oh, of course."

Elizabeth turned to go, then paused as Marlene said quietly, "Lady Elizabeth, I hope you find out who did it. Sam Cutter's a good bloke and our Polly thinks the world of him. I know he's not the one that did it. Please help him."

Elizabeth smiled. "I'll do my best, Marlene. That's all I can promise."

Marlene seemed relieved. "That's all I can ask, m'm."

It could have been Sam's jeep that Marlene heard as she was falling asleep, Elizabeth thought, as she left the little shop. Then again, Marlene could have imagined it in her anxiety to help clear Sam's name. So far, all she had were words, opinions, speculations.

The one person who had a definite motive and opportunity was Sam Cutter. The only other person who might have had a reason to want Kenny dead had apparently been cleared by the investigators. Unless she came up with some solid proof, Sam could be in serious trouble.

Her short visit to the police station to talk to Constable George Dalrymple didn't help at all.

"Can't get near the bloomin' place, your ladyship," George grumbled. "After the initial investigation, they suggested Sid and I leave it all up to them to find the murderer. Like we were stupid or something. I'll have them know I was a bloody good policeman in my day. Just because I was retired before the war broke out doesn't mean I've lost me marbles, now does it."

"Not that you had that many to start with," Sid observed from the doorway of the barren little office.

"Shut up, Sid." George gave Elizabeth a smile of apology. "He got up too early this morning, your ladyship. Gets a touch bilious, he does. Been in the toilet half the morning."

Sid's cheeks flamed red, but fortunately he kept his retort to himself.

Having heard more than she wanted to know, Elizabeth said hurriedly, "Did you see anything in the bell tower that might have helped discover who killed Kenny Morris?"

George looked wary. "Even if I did, m'm, I wouldn't be at liberty to tell you."

Well used to playing this game, Elizabeth said brightly, "Of course not, George. I wouldn't dream of putting you on a spot like that."

"Thank you, your ladyship. Much obliged, I'm sure."

"There's just one thing I'd like to know, George. Of course you don't have to tell me anything, but if I'm right, you could sort of nod, perhaps, or shake your head?"

"He's very good at nodding and shaking, your ladyship," Sid said, with a snide glance at his partner. "Especially when he doesn't know what the heck he's talking about. Which is just about all of the time."

George gave Sid a look that should have cut him in half. "Don't you have work to do?"

"All right, keep your hair on." Sid nodded at Elizabeth. "TTFN, your ladyship."

Elizabeth stared after him. "TTFN? What on earth did that mean?"

George shook his head. "Oh, it means ta-ta for now. It's from Itma, one of them shows on the wireless."

Thoroughly mystified, Elizabeth stared at him. *"Itma?"*

"Stands for *It's That Man Again*. Tommy Handley, his name is." He grinned. "It's a really good laugh, your ladyship."

"Really," Elizabeth said faintly. "It seems that the Americans are not the only ones speaking an odd form of English these days."

"Sign of the times, I suppose, m'm."

Deciding it was time she got back to business, Elizabeth said briskly, "Yes, well, about this unfortunate incident in the bell tower. I understand a knife was found near the body."

George's expression turned wary again. Slowly he nodded his head.

"I don't remember seeing it when we discovered Kenny's body. Was the knife close to the body?"

Her answer was a firm shake of the head this time.

"Far away?"

George lifted his hand and wagged it from side to side.

"Would you say five feet? Ten? Fifteen?" Finally getting the answer she needed, she added quickly, "The drops of blood on the floor—were they close to where the knife was found?"

"Pretty close," George said, then clamped his mouth shut.

"Nothing else was found?"

George shook his head.

Not sure what she was going to make of this information, Elizabeth thanked him and left. If only she could get into the bell tower and take a good look around, she might be able to come up with an idea of where to look next. Right now, there didn't seem to be much else she could do.

On the wild chance that the guard had left the bell tower, she rode down to the churchyard and parked her motorcycle outside the gates. Her hopes were dashed immediately by the sight of the uniformed officer seated in the doorway, his nose buried deep in a book.

At least he couldn't stop her wandering around the churchyard, she decided, though what she expected to find after her last fruitless search she had no idea. Nevertheless, she set off down the gravel path, trying not to look too conspicuous when the American officer glanced up at her.

The setting sun shone brightly, despite the lateness of the hour. Now that most of the leaves had departed from the trees, they looked quite forlorn. Birds' nests, long abandoned by their occupants, dotted the bare branches, starkly visible now that their green, leafy camouflage had disappeared.

Gazing up at a magpie nest jammed in between two branches of an ancient gnarled oak, Elizabeth was intrigued to spot something gleaming in the untidy wad of mud and twigs. The scavenger bird had a penchant for making off with valuables, and her curiosity was immediately aroused.

The tree stood very close to the back wall of the church, with its branches extending over the roof. The nest was about halfway up the tree, easily accessed with the help of a convenient drainpipe and several sturdy, low-lying limbs protruding near the base of the thick trunk.

Directly below the target branches, a ground-level basement window also offered a foothold, since its thick frame extended a couple of inches from the wall.

Elizabeth glanced around and assured herself she was completely alone and hidden from the road, as well as the vicarage and the bell tower. Then, hitching up the skirt of her wool frock, she placed a foot on the window ledge, grasped the drainpipe, and hauled herself into the tree.

She had only to clamber up three branches before she could reach inside the nest. Her fingers encountered broken eggshells, acorns, and something she didn't want to inspect too closely, before she grasped something smooth and oblong. Withdrawing the object, she caught her breath. It was a beautiful silver comb, the kind one wore in the hair on special occasions. Obviously quite old, with its ornate handle studded with tiny diamonds, it had to be worth a lot of money, not to mention sentimental value to its owner.

Judging from the gray hairs still attached to the teeth of the comb, whoever had lost it was apparently elderly, and probably devastated by the loss.

Holding the precious object tightly in one hand, Elizabeth began the descent to the ground. Unfortunately she snagged one of her gloves on a small spike, and in an effort to free herself, tore a hole in it, dropping the comb in the process.

Irritated with herself, she climbed down from the tree and brushed the pieces of bark from her dress. The brown stains left behind would no doubt evoke intense irritation from Violet, especially since the dry cleaners in North Horsham had closed down almost a year ago.

After searching for a few minutes around the base of the tree, Elizabeth spotted the comb lying in the deep grass at the side of the basement window. As she bent to retrieve it, she noticed several gray hairs trapped in the top of the window frame, apparently deposited there by the wind. The comb must have slipped out of the owner's head as she walked along the path that led close to the wall around the church. The magpie, having been attracted by the sun sparkling on the diamonds, would have swooped down and carried the comb back to its nest.

It was such a distinctive piece that Elizabeth hoped the vicar might recognize it as belonging to one of his parishioners. She found him in the garden of the vicarage, raking the leaves from his trim lawn.

After greeting her effusively, he took the comb from her and examined it. "I don't remember seeing it on any of my congregation," he said, turning it one way and then the other. "I do have many elderly worshipers, of course. I'd like to keep it for a while, if I may. Perhaps I can find the owner. It's such a lovely piece."

Elizabeth smiled. "It is, indeed. Thank you, Vicar. I hope you find to whom it belongs. I'd hate to lose it if it were mine."

"I'll do my best." The vicar peered at her, his eyes almost invisible behind his thick glasses. "I suppose you know that one of your Americans has been arrested for the murder in the bell tower."

Elizabeth wasn't sure she liked her uninvited guests referred to as "her" Americans, but she merely nodded. "Sam Cutter, yes. He happens to be a good friend of my assistant, Polly Barnett."

The vicar raised his shaggy white eyebrows. "Polly is your assistant now?"

"It's a long story, Vicar. The point is, no one who knows Sam Cutter believes he is capable of such a violent deed."

"Ah, who knows what we are capable of when driven by one of the seven deadly sins. Man is an unpredictable creature, Lady Elizabeth, and while I hesitate to single any one out, I must confess that I find these American fellows a different breed, indeed."

Depressed, Elizabeth had to agree. Still, just because they were different didn't mean they were any more capable of murder than anyone else, she argued silently on her way back to the manor. Take Earl, for instance. He was utterly unlike any man she had ever met—in his manner, in his attitude, and especially in the way he treated a woman.

Unlike the men with whom she had previously been associated, her ex-husband in particular, Earl made her feel that he was truly interested in what she had to say, that he respected her opinion, and that he considered her an equal, a person in her own right, rather than simply an appendage of her lord and master. She appreciated that very much. It was a large part of the reason she was so taken with him.

If all Americans treated British women that way, she reflected, as she sailed up the long, tree-lined driveway, it was really no wonder the British men were being left out in the cold. And no wonder that Polly was so devastated by Sam Cutter's arrest.

She still had no clear idea of whether she considered Sam innocent or guilty. As the vicar had said, who knows what a man is capable of when under duress. One thing she did know. She was not about to let an innocent man be punished for a crime he didn't commit, or allow the true culprit to escape.

Somehow she had to find the proof she needed. If Sam was guilty, then he would have to accept the consequences and Polly would just have to live with it. But if Sam Cutter was innocent, then it was up to her to find out exactly what went on in the bell tower that night. Not only because Earl had asked her for help, but because if there was one thing in the world she would not tolerate, it was injustice. Especially in her own village.

CHAPTER

❧ 11 ❧

Elizabeth spent the next day organizing the preparations for the Stately Homes tour on Saturday. It had been at least a year or two since anyone had toured the Manor House, and every room, every nook and cranny had to be inspected, thoroughly cleaned, and rearranged, if necessary.

Heavy clouds had brought rain, and the damp chill in the house seemed to penetrate to the bone. Violet rushed around, huffing and puffing like an aging dragon, while Polly grumbled and complained at having to spend her time doing housework instead of being where she wanted to be—in the office.

Bessie had passed on Elizabeth's request for help to her three assistants, and Janet, an exuberant young brunette with aspirations of living in America, had jumped at the opportunity. She spent more time bombarding Polly with questions about the Yanks than paying attention to her duties, adding to Polly's frustrations.

Desmond kept popping in to ask Elizabeth what she wanted pruned, thinned out, cut down, or left alone, and left behind huge muddy footprints in the kitchen, while Martin disappeared altogether, no doubt to escape the massive disruption of his daily life.

Elizabeth, under pressure from Polly's muttering, put in a call to the Labour Exchange in London. The woman who answered her assured her she would have no trouble in filling the position of housemaid at the manor, and promised to call her as soon as she had some applicants ready to come down for an interview. Wondering what she had let herself in for, Elizabeth returned to the fray.

By nightfall the Manor House was sparkling, and ready to greet its visitors the following day. In honor of the occasion, Violet laid the fires in all of the fireplaces, and set light to them all.

The warmth creeping through the hallways warmed every corner on every floor, and lifted Elizabeth's sagging spirits. As she sat warming her toes in front of the glowing coals in the quiet peace of the library, she wished she'd had the courage to invite Earl to share a glass of sherry with her. There was something so romantic about a fire in the fireplace, which was precisely why she hadn't given in to her inappropriate impulse.

Instead she rested her aching muscles, and watched the puppies sleeping in front of the flickering flames. Tomorrow would be another long day. And still she wasn't any closer to solving the mystery of the bell tower murder.

The heavy downpour had dwindled down to a light shower or two by the next morning. Seated at her usual place at the breakfast table, Elizabeth stared in surprise as Martin entered the kitchen. He was attired in a black morning coat that had probably fit him well a half century ago, but was now sagging pitifully on his frail frame.

"Good morning, madam." He patted his chest and peered at her over his glasses. "Quite impressive, even if I do say so myself."

"You look like you've been put through a wringer and hung out on a line to dry," Violet observed from her spot at the stove.

Elizabeth frowned at her, then smiled at her butler. "You look very nice, Martin. To what do we owe all this unaccustomed magnificence?"

Martin raised his thin eyebrows. "Have you forgotten, madam? The Manor House has been prepared for weekend visitors. The master and Lady Wellsborough will be expecting me to look my best to receive their honorable guests. I shall not let them down."

"Oh, crikey," Violet muttered. "Here he goes again."

"There won't be weekend visitors, Martin," Elizabeth said gently. "My parents died two years ago, remember? You look very impressive, I must say, but I really think a suit would be more appropriate for the occasion."

He looked puzzled. "And what occasion would that be, madam?"

Elizabeth sighed. "Sit down, Martin, and have your breakfast. You'll feel better when you eat."

Martin bowed as well as his aging bones would allow. "May I have your permission to join you at the table, madam?"

"You may, Martin."

"Thank you, madam."

"Not at all, Martin." She watched him with a worried frown as he eased down onto his chair. This would not be a good day for Martin to have one of his bouts of confusion. Violet and Polly would need all the help they could get to keep things in order as it was.

She waited for him to settle himself, then said gently,

"You do know that we are having a group of people tour the house today, don't you, Martin?"

"Of course, madam." Martin lifted his empty teacup and peered at it. "Did I drink my tea already?"

"I haven't poured it yet." Violet slammed the lid down on a large saucepan with a loud clatter. "I've only got one pair of hands. I can't do everything at once."

Elizabeth's frown deepened. "Is something the matter, Violet?"

"I've just got a lot on my mind, that's all." Violet spooned hot porridge into two plates and brought them to the table. "There. Milk's in the jug. Just be careful with the sugar."

Martin stared at his plate. "Porridge? Where's my eggs and bacon? What about my sausage?"

Violet whirled on him, her fists digging into her hips. "For your information, Mr. High and Mighty, there's a bloody war on. Eat it and be glad you've got a warm meal inside you. There are thousands out there who would give their right arm for a bowl of hot porridge."

Martin muttered something under his breath and picked up his spoon.

Wisely, Elizabeth decided not to comment on the somewhat meager breakfast after the sumptuous meals they had previously enjoyed. She ate the porridge in silence, trying not to notice when Martin dropped a blob of sticky oatmeal on the lapel of his coat.

"Has Polly arrived yet?" she asked Violet, when the housekeeper collected the empty plates. "I need to go over a few things with her before the tour gets here."

She winced when Violet dropped the dishes in the sink with a crash that threatened to smash them into pieces. "She got here an hour ago. Went straight into the office, she did. She's walking around with a face as long as a poker. That girl has been moping about ever since those investigators picked up her boyfriend. If you ask me, she's too blinking young to be worrying about boys. Watching her miserable face is getting on my nerves, that it is."

It was Elizabeth's considered opinion that something far more significant than Polly's long face was getting on Violet's nerves, but she knew better than to ask right then. The best time to tackle her housekeeper would be after the tour was over, and things settled down again. Until then, there was much to be done.

Brian Forrester arrived precisely at one o'clock. Watching the tourists awkwardly descend from the coach in the driveway, Elizabeth was concerned that most of them looked too frail to be walking around the manor for two hours. But then, Mr. Forrester seemed to have lots of experience with elderly people, and no doubt knew what he was doing.

Thus assured, she retired to the office to catch up on some paperwork that had been sadly neglected of late. Since Violet would be fully occupied with the tour, Elizabeth had offered to keep the dogs with her until everyone had left.

Listening to them scamper around the desk was rather distracting, but she made herself concentrate and tried to ignore the scuffling, barking, and scratching going on in various parts of the room.

She had been at work for no more than ten minutes when the door of her office opened and a dumpy little woman stood in the doorway. She wore a black hat with a brim that curled over one eye, making it necessary to tilt her head to see out from under it.

"Oh," she said with a little laugh, "I was looking for the lavatory. Is it in here?"

"Oh, please, shut the door," Elizabeth cried, but it was too late. The moment the puppies sensed freedom, they were out the door and off to parts unknown.

"Oh, I'm dreadfully sorry," the woman said, belatedly closing the door. "I thought this was the bathroom."

Elizabeth put down her pen. "I'm sorry, but this is

not the bathroom. If you ask a member of my staff, one of them will be happy to escort you to the right place."

"Oh, dear." The woman looked over her shoulder. "I'm afraid I've lost everyone. I don't know where they've gone."

Realizing that she could hardly send the poor woman wandering off on her own, Elizabeth reluctantly rose to her feet. What on earth was Brian Forrester doing that he didn't notice one of his charges was missing?

"Come along," she said briskly, "I'll show you where it is." With the woman in tow she marched along the hallway, and came face to face with Martin. Her butler clung to the arm of a little man whose face was almost hidden by a cloud of white whiskers.

"Ah, there you are, madam," Martin cried out when he saw her. "I must ask that you call the constables at once. I have apprehended an intruder."

The little man glared at Martin. " 'Ere, watch who you're calling an intruder. Let go me bloody arm."

"That's not an intruder," the woman piped up. "That's our Ernie."

"Martin," Elizabeth said sternly, "let the man go at once. He's part of the group touring the manor today. Remember? I told you they were coming."

Martin peered at her over his glasses. "Tour?"

"Yes, you bloody nincompoop," the little man muttered. "I told you I was here on a tour." He glared at Elizabeth. "Bleeding barmy, he is."

Martin seemed to grow an inch. "Any more of that language, my good man, and I'll throw you out myself. This is Lady Elizabeth Hartleigh Compton you are addressing, and I won't stand for that kind of language in her presence."

The little man appeared unimpressed, but the woman gave a little shriek. "Oh, my, a real lady. Never thought I'd meet a real lady in my whole life."

"Martin, take that man back to where you found him."

Elizabeth turned to the woman. "The lavatory is right down the hall to the left."

The woman curtsied, nearly toppling over in the process. "Thank you, your ladyship, though I think it might be a little too late now."

"Oh, dear, I certainly hope not." Elizabeth watched the woman hurry down the hallway, then caught sight of one of the puppies racing up the stairs to the east wing.

Abandoning Martin's captive to his fate, she sprinted for the stairs. Violet had hung a green velvet ribbon across the stairwell to prevent the tourists from wandering into the Americans' quarters. Elizabeth ducked under it and chased up the steps after the puppy.

Bedlam reigned in the Manor House for the rest of the afternoon. Brian Forrester seemed incapable of controlling his group, and people roamed all over the house without proper supervision. Polly and Violet were kept hopping, running in different directions to herd the strays back to the fold.

One of the tourists put on the suit of armor and became trapped inside it. Desmond had to be summoned to rescue the unfortunate man. Both puppies disappeared and it took Elizabeth over an hour of searching before she eventually found them asleep under one of the cots in the officers' quarters.

Brian Forrester was also missing for a while. When Violet found him in the wine cellar, he'd already polished off two bottles of excellent Beaujolais. As for Martin, he locked himself in his room and refused to come out.

By the time the group of weary and confused tourists had been rounded up and loaded on the coach, Elizabeth was exhausted, Violet wasn't speaking to anyone, and Polly looked as if her face would crack if she smiled.

As she stood at the window of the library and watched the coach roll down the driveway, Elizabeth was absolutely and positively certain she would never allow another tour of her home.

Basking in the blessed peace that had descended over the manor, she headed for the conservatory, where she intended to finish off the bottle of sherry she'd opened the day before. For once she didn't even feel like talking to Earl. She needed to be alone, with nothing more pressing to think about than how soon she could sink into bed.

She had just poured herself a generous glass of sherry when she heard a tap on the door. Violet poked her head around and, in the same grumpy tone she'd used all day, said, "Mr. Forrester wants a word with you."

Elizabeth stared at her in amazement. "I thought they left."

Violet rolled her eyes. "*They* left. *He* didn't."

Elizabeth put down her glass. "Tell him I've retired for the evening. He can ring me tomorrow. No, not tomorrow, it's Sunday. Tell him to ring me on Monday."

"I tried telling him," Violet said, gritting her teeth. "He won't listen. He won't leave until he's spoken to you."

Fighting back a surge of resentment, Elizabeth lifted her hands in defeat. "All right, I'll speak to him. But not in here."

"I didn't think so. He's waiting in the library. I'll show him into the office when you get there."

Violet withdrew her head, and Elizabeth took a long sip of her sherry before following her housekeeper out the door. As they walked together down the hallway, she laid a hand on Violet's arm. "Have I offended you in some way, Violet?"

Violet's fierce frown smoothed out at once. "Oh, no, Lizzie, it's not you. Just a lot of things happening all at once, that's all."

Relieved, Elizabeth said quickly, "Violet, I'm so sorry about today. I know how hard it was for you and Polly.

We'll just have to find some other way to raise money. I'll ring London on Monday to take us off the Estate Tours, I promise."

Violet wearily nodded. "Whatever you say, Lizzie." She paused at the library door. "Be careful of this man. I don't trust him."

Elizabeth smiled. "Don't worry, Violet. I can handle him."

"I bloomin' hope so."

Elizabeth walked on to the office, while behind her the housekeeper announced with some belligerence, "Lady Elizabeth will see you now in her office."

Seating herself at her desk, Elizabeth prepared to deal with whatever Brian Forrester had to say to her.

It was obvious, the moment he entered the room, that the wine had gone straight to his head. He swayed on his feet, and he appeared unable to focus his gaze on her as he stood in front of her desk. His tucked his thumbs into his waistcoat. "Just wanted to thank you, Lady 'Lizabeth, for allowing me and my old-agers into your magnifishent home."

"My pleasure," Elizabeth murmured, hoping the blatant lie sounded at least marginally sincere.

"Yes, indeed." Forrester waved a hand expansively at the dark paneled walls. "Nice place you have here. I'd enjoy an office like thish."

Elizabeth glanced pointedly at the Westminster clock on the mantelpiece. "Is there something I can help you with, Mr. Forrester?"

"Huh? Oh, no, not really. Just wanted to thank you."

"Then consider me thanked."

Some of her irritation must have sounded in her voice, since he narrowed his eyes and leaned forward with his hands on her desk. "Too bad we couldn't shee all of the house, though. Some of my people feel shortchanged. Trush the Yanks to barge in where they're not wanted. Bloody intruders, that's what I call them."

Reminding herself that she was a lady, Elizabeth said coolly, "Yes, well, if that's all, Mr. Forrester—"

"That's not all, your ladyship. Not by a long chalk. No, shur. I'm sick and tired of these Yanks comin' in and taking over everything. As far as I'm concerned, the only good Yank is a dead Yank, and I'm jolly glad that bashtard got his neck wrung in the bell tower. One lesh to worry about, that's what I shay."

Incensed, Elizabeth soared to her feet. "That's quite enough, Mr. Forrester. You are no longer welcome in my home, and I would greatly appreciate it if you would take your leave at once."

Forrester grinned unpleasantly. "Washamatta, hit a raw spot, did I? Surely, Lady 'Lizabeth, you're not one of those Yankee bait I keep hearing about?"

Unfortunately for Forrester, the door flew open at that moment, revealing a very tall, very angry American in the uniform of the United States Army Air Force. Although he managed to keep his voice low, the lethal note was unmistakable. "You, sir, are leaving. Right now."

Forrester's gloating expression changed to apprehension. He slowly straightened, then turned to face his opponent, while Elizabeth gazed at Earl in grateful relief.

"Who's going to make me," Forrester said nastily, with apparent disregard for his safety.

Earl took a step forward. "I was hoping you'd say something like that." His hand shot out and grabbed Forrester by the scruff of the neck. "It'll be a pleasure to escort you outside, Mr. Forrester."

"Get your damn hands off me, shur!" Forrester roared. "I know what you are. You're nothing but shcum, the lot of you. Go back where you belong, you—"

Whatever he was going to say was cut off by Earl's hand covering his mouth. "Be right back," Earl said grimly, then hustled the spluttering man out the door.

Elizabeth could hear Forrester complaining all the way down the hall, then the noise gradually faded into silence. She sat down hard on her chair, and realized she was trembling. What an awful man. And how gallant of Earl to remove him like that.

Overcome in her awe of the commanding way he'd taken charge of the situation and dealt with it, she clasped her hands together to stop them shaking. Most impressive. Heroic. Exciting, really.

She sat for a while, trying to calm her shattered nerves, reliving again and again the moment when Earl burst into the room. That moment would dwell in her memory for as long as she lived.

She'd managed to compose herself by the time Earl returned. Smiling at him, she pulled herself to her feet. "Thank you for coming to my rescue. You seem to do be doing that rather a lot lately."

He grinned at her. "My pleasure, your ladyship. Just part of my duties here."

"Somehow I doubt that defending the lady of the manor from obnoxious tour guides is listed in your duty roster, Major."

"Well, it should be." His gaze sharpened in concern. "Are you all right? You looked a bit peaked."

She managed a shaky laugh. "Just exhausted, that's all. It's been a hectic day."

"So I hear. Violet filled me in on the day's events. Sounds like you all had a fun day."

Elizabeth pulled a face. "The only ones who really had fun were George and Gracie." She hesitated, then throwing caution to the wind, added, "Would you care to join me in the conservatory for a glass of sherry?"

"Tell you what." He opened the door and ushered her through with a warm hand on her back. "I left a bottle of brandy down in the kitchen with Violet. Why don't we have a drop of that instead."

She sighed with pleasure. "Major, while I frown on accepting merchandise from the base, in this case I'll be happy to make an exception."

Seated in the conservatory a few minutes later, she had to admit the brandy tasted marvelous and did wonders for her sense of well-being. Or maybe it was the sight of Earl seated across from her that made her feel so utterly content.

"I hope we've seen the last of that man," she said, transferring her gaze to the dancing flames in the fireplace. "Such an unpleasant creature."

"So I hear. Sam was so sure he was the one who killed Kenny Morris."

"I was rather hoping he'd be arrested for the murder myself." Elizabeth held her brandy glass in both hands and swirled the golden liquid around to warm it. "I was quite surprised when he rang to say he was coming back down here."

"From what I heard, Forrester told the investigators his car broke down near the church after the poker game. He told them he walked back to the pub that night, leaving his car by the side of the road, then went back the next morning to fix it himself before driving back to London."

"And they are convinced he's telling the truth?"

Earl shrugged. "Hard to say. The problem, I guess, is that it's tough to prove, one way or the other."

"But they can't prove it was Sam, either."

"Maybe not. But they're going to be a lot more careful about accusing a British citizen of murder than they are holding under suspicion an officer in the United States Army Air Force."

"I suppose so. How long can they hold Sam without a trial?"

"As long as they want, I reckon."

She met his gaze. "Who do you think is more capable of murder?"

"I honestly don't know. Forrester's a jerk, but I don't know if he'd kill someone any more than Sam would."

"What we need is proof."

"That would help."

Pure instinct made her lean forward and touch his hand. "I'll do my best to find it for you."

He turned his palm up and clasped her fingers for a precious moment or two. "Stay out of trouble, Elizabeth. I'd never forgive myself if something happened to you."

And that, she thought happily, was the very best thing he could possibly have said.

CHAPTER

❧ 12 ❧

As Elizabeth left the church the next morning, the Reverend Roland Cumberland beckoned her to one side. "I'm giving you this back, Lady Elizabeth," he said, handing her the silver comb. "I've asked all my parishioners if anyone recognizes it, and no one seems to have seen it before. Perhaps it was dropped by a visitor in the village. In any case, I think you should have it."

"Thank you, Vicar." Elizabeth opened her handbag and slipped the comb inside. "If anyone should ask for it, I'll be happy to return it."

The vicar nodded. "I don't think anyone will. Not after all this time. You haven't heard anything more about the murder, I suppose?"

"I'm sorry to say I haven't." Elizabeth glanced over at the bell tower. "Are they still on guard over there?"

"Not for much longer, thank heavens." The vicar peered up at the bells. "I was told this morning that the tower would be vacated by the investigators by the end of the week."

"How nice. Then you won't have to worry about summoning your congregation to worship."

She was on her way back to the Manor House when an idea came to her. After precariously turning her motorcycle around in a narrow lane, she headed back the way she had come. She had noticed Marlene and Polly in the crowd leaving the church, and hoped to catch up with them before they had time to reach their house.

It wasn't long before she spotted the sisters walking along the coast road, accompanied by their mother. All three women turned to look at her as she roared up behind them and spluttered to a stop.

Polly looked worried, and asked immediately, "Is Sam all right, your ladyship?"

Elizabeth smiled. "As far as I know, Polly. At least if he's confined to barracks, you know he's not flying over Germany right now."

Polly nodded, though she didn't appear to consider that much compensation.

Edna tutted. "Really, I don't know what's got into the girl, your ladyship. Always worrying about a blinking Yank. If you ask me, they're big enough and bold enough to take care of themselves."

"I doubt if the Americans are any less vulnerable than we are when it comes to risking their lives in the skies," Elizabeth commented.

Edna had the grace to sound contrite when she said hurriedly, "Oh, of course, m'm. You know I didn't mean anything by it."

Elizabeth took the comb out of her handbag and showed it to Marlene. "I found this in the churchyard a few days ago. I was wondering if perhaps you might recognize it as belonging to one of your customers?"

Watched curiously by Polly and her mother, Marlene took the comb and turned it over in her hands. "It's not one of my customers, I can tell you that. I know that nobody what comes into my shop would have hair in this condition." She pointed to the gray hairs in the teeth. "Look at it. It's as dry as straw."

"And you are absolutely sure you've never seen the comb before?"

"Never set eyes on it until this moment, your ladyship. I'd know it again in an instant if I had."

Thanking her, Elizabeth took the comb and dropped it into her handbag.

"I want to thank you, m'm," Edna said earnestly, "for giving our Polly a job in your office. She's been a different girl these past weeks, that she has. At least she was until this latest murder business with the Yank."

Polly scowled. "Aw, Ma, don't go on about it."

"Well, I must say, your daughter is doing an excellent job," Elizabeth assured her, and was immediately rewarded with a dazzling smile from Polly.

"Am I, m'm? Really? I do try hard, really I do."

"I know you do, Polly. I want you to know I rang London the other day. They'll be sending down some replacements for interviews soon. That should make things easier for you."

Polly beamed. "Thank you, m'm. I won't let you down, I promise."

"Yes, well, now I must be off." Bidding them all farewell, Elizabeth started the engine and took off into the brisk sea wind. Another dead end. Much as she hated to admit defeat, it didn't seem as though she could be of any help to Earl and Sam Cutter after all.

Her spirits sank even lower when she returned to the manor to find Violet still in a foul mood. After watching her housekeeper smack bowls of soup on the table hard enough to spill their contents, she decided it was time to intervene.

"This smells very good, Violet," she said, picking up her spoon. "What is it?"

"Vegetable soup," Violet muttered. "All I could manage today. It's getting impossible to find decent food in the shop anymore."

Elizabeth refrained from commenting, though she did wonder if perhaps the source of under-the-counter goods had finally dried up, which would explain the return to frugal meals and the demise of Violet's good temper.

Making up her mind to ask her housekeeper later, she finished off the soup, then retired to her office to spend the afternoon catching up on her paperwork.

"Get that hair dry before you go out, my girl," Edna yelled, as Polly headed up the narrow hallway to the front door. "You'll catch your death of pneumonia if you don't."

"Aw, Ma!" Polly halted, scowling at her mother over her shoulder. "I washed it nearly an hour ago. It's got to be dry by now."

Edna marched up to her young daughter and laid a hand on her dark tresses. "Exactly what I thought, it's sopping wet. Get your blinking head down in front of that fireplace and dry it all off this minute."

Grumbling and complaining, Polly threw off her coat and slunk into the living room, where flames licked at a pile of glowing coals in the fireplace. She sank to her knees and lowered her chin until her hair hung like a silky curtain in front of the blue-tinged flames.

"Don't know why we can't have one of them hair dryers like Marlene's got in her shop," she muttered.

Edna, who had followed Polly into the room to make sure the girl did as she was ordered, let out a loud snort. "Just where do you think we'd get the money for one of those machines? Must cost a blinking fortune."

"Marlene could snitch one from the shop. They'd never know where it had gone."

"Watch your tongue, my girl. I won't have you talking about stealing like some common little guttersnipe. What on earth has got into you, Polly? It's them Yanks, that's what it is. Teaching you all this stuff about stealing and murder and the like. They all ought to be locked up, that's what I say."

"Oh, yeah?" Polly tilted her head so she could look at her mother through her parted hair. "Then who's going to shoot down the Germans for us?"

Edna tossed her head. "Our boys are quite capable of shooting down Germans. We don't need no Yanks."

"If it hadn't been for the Yanks," Polly said bluntly, "we'd all be dead. The Germans would have flattened this village by now."

"I never heard such nonsense—" Edna broke off as the loud rapping on the door echoed down the hallway. "Now who could that be?"

"You won't know unless you answer it." Polly let out her breath on a frustrated sigh as her mother hurried from the room. It seemed like she could do nothing right for her ma anymore. Ever since she started going with Sam, Ma had been on her back, nagging and carrying on about it.

Polly swung her head to the other side to expose the wet side of it to the fire. Well, no matter what Ma said or did, she was never going to give up on Sam. Not even if he was sent back to America. She'd write to him, and stay true to him forever. Even if she never saw him again.

Before she could stop it a tear rolled down her cheek and splashed onto the fireplace. She dashed away the next one with the back of her hand. It wouldn't do to let Ma see her crying.

The sound of voices in the hallway reached her ears and she raised her head. Ma was talking to a man. For a minute her heart stopped. Surely those investigators weren't coming back to talk to her again? The man's voice grew louder, and she froze, her heart skipping madly now.

It sounded like Sam's voice.

Hardly daring to believe it, she scrambled to her feet and stared at the open doorway, afraid to move. Then a tall figure filled the frame. With an ear-splitting scream of joy she threw herself into Sam's waiting arms.

Earl stopped by Elizabeth's office on his way to a briefing that afternoon. As always, she was pleasurably disturbed by his presence, and overlooked the fact that he displaced her stack of unpaid bills when he perched a hip on her desk.

Normally she would never allow such a lack of decorum. In fact, had it been anyone but Earl, she would have been highly offended that anyone would take such liberties as to sit on her desk. After all, what good were chairs if one didn't use them.

Somehow, because it was Earl, none of that seemed to matter. He was American, and if that was what Americans did, then it was all right with her. Just as long as he used the proper respect in public. Which he always did, of course.

If she were totally honest with herself, she'd admit that she found his familiarity rather stimulating. Under any other circumstances, she might have quite enjoyed flying in the face of convention. Unfortunately, she owed it to her ancestors to act with the proper decorum at all times. There were definite disadvantages to being the lady of the manor.

"Just wanted to let you know there might be a break in the case," Earl told her, as she gingerly moved her inkwell away from his thigh. "It looks as if Kenny Morris was dealing in black market merchandise. The investigators learned that he was transporting supplies stolen from the base to a contact in the village—probably a local."

Thoroughly jolted, Elizabeth stared at him. "Kenny Morris had a contact? Do they know who it is?"

Earl picked up a pencil and began doodling on her blotter. "Not yet, but they're working on it. They're real anxious to talk to the guy. The other good news is that they've released Sam Cutter from CB. I guess they didn't have enough evidence to hold him after all."

"Oh, I'm so glad. Polly will be so relieved."

"He's not out of the woods yet, by any means. Until we can find out who killed Kenny, Sam will still be under suspicion. But at least he's back on duty. Though I'm not sure he's any better off."

Something in his voice sent a chill through Elizabeth. "Is something going on?"

"Nothing I can talk about." He threw down the pencil and got up from the desk. "I'm still hoping we can all make the cricket lesson tomorrow evening."

"Good." She managed a smile as she rose to see him out. "I believe Percy Bodkins will be there, and Alfie from the Tudor Arms, since it's his night off. Oh, and Captain Carbunkle has promised to offer his services."

Earl raised his eyebrows. "Army captain?"

"Merchant navy, retired. He used to captain a cricket eleven at one time, I believe. He's on the village council. He's a bit of a chatterbox, and can bore you to tears with his sea stories, but he means well."

Earl grinned. "Sounds like a blast. I'm looking forward to it." He glanced at his watch, then opened the door. "Gotta run. Will you be there tomorrow?"

"I wouldn't miss it for the world."

"Till tomorrow, then."

He pulled on his cap and turned to go, pausing when she said urgently, "Earl?"

He looked back at her, his eyes questioning.

"Please, be careful."

"Always." He touched the peak of his cap, and then he was gone, leaving an empty ache of worry in her heart.

She sat for several minutes at her desk, trying to concentrate on the village councillors' suggestion that they reinstate the bonfire and fireworks celebrations on Guy Fawkes night. The annual tradition had been halted, thanks to the risk of enemy bombers strafing the villagers who would be illuminated in the light of the flames.

Although the threat had diminished somewhat since the Blitz, the blackout was still in full force, and Elizabeth could not justify taking the risk for the sake of a few fireworks.

She was having a good deal of trouble, however, wording her objections without raising unnecessary alarm. Finally she gave up, acknowledging that the concern uppermost in her mind was not the possibility of German bombers being attracted to the area by the fireworks, as much as the very real possibility that the contact receiving stolen goods from Kenny Morris could actually be her own housekeeper.

Until a few minutes ago, she hadn't dreamed there could be a connection between Kenny's murder and the flow of black market goods. Until then, the whole thing had seemed quite trivial, in the light of everything else going on, but now it had all suddenly turned serious. If Violet was involved, then it could be catastrophic for her.

There was only one way to find out. Elizabeth laid down her pen and, in spite of her concern, smiled at Earl's drawing of a Spitfire on her pink blotter. That was one piece of blotting paper she would never throw away.

She found Violet resting with her feet up by the stove, a magazine on her lap while her chin nodded on her chest. Her snore ended in a snort when Elizabeth touched her on the shoulder.

Instantly awake, Violet swung her feet to the floor. "What is it? Not Martin, is it?"

Elizabeth sat down opposite her. "Martin is fine, as far as I know. I want to talk to you about all the extra food you've been serving up lately. Food that should be on ration."

Violet's face closed up. "I've been saving up the coupons, that's all."

"Violet, we could never have enough coupons to provide the amount of meat, eggs, and sugar you've been giving us lately. I need to know the truth. Where did you get all this food?"

"I've been trading with some of the villagers. Lots of people don't use up their coupons. Some of them don't eat meat and some can't afford it."

It was time for some straight talking, Elizabeth decided. "Violet, the American investigators have discovered that Kenny Morris was supplying someone in the village with goods stolen from the base. They are looking for that contact right now. If you are connected to this in any way, you could well be involved in a murder investigation. You must tell me the truth, Violet. I can't help you if I don't know what you've done."

Violet's eyes had been growing wider throughout this speech. As Elizabeth paused, she burst out, "I never had anything to do with Kenny Morris. I swear on my life I didn't."

Wanting desperately to believe her, Elizabeth demanded, "Then where did you get all that food?"

"I promised I wouldn't tell anyone. I swore I wouldn't tell."

"Violet, you have to tell me. Someone has been killed, possibly because of this black market thing, and you could be in an awful lot of trouble. You must tell me."

For a long moment Violet stared at her, then, her voice low, she muttered, "It was Percy. I got the extra stuff under the counter from Percy."

Elizabeth briefly closed her eyes, remembering again the green straw she'd seen in Percy's display counter. "I was afraid of that."

"You don't think Percy killed that man, do you?" Violet jumped up, sending the magazine to the floor. "He wouldn't hurt a fly. Not Percy. I've known him since we were kids. More than fifty years. He couldn't kill a man like that. He couldn't even go after that German pilot that landed here a few weeks ago. He's dead against the war. He's always telling me that violence doesn't solve anything."

"Calm down, Violet, I'm not accusing Percy of anything." Elizabeth got up from her chair and held her chilly hands close to the stove to warm them. "He is obviously involved in all of this, however, and the investigators are bound to question him."

"Are you going to tell them?"

Elizabeth avoided Violet's accusing eyes. "Not until I've had a chance to talk to him. I'll stop by the shop in the morning. I have to speak to him anyway about the cricket lesson tomorrow night."

"You won't tell him I told you? I swore I wouldn't."

Elizabeth shook her head. "It really doesn't matter, Violet. Percy was doing something wrong. He knew the risk he was taking. Sooner or later the truth would have come out."

"Maybe not," Violet said soberly. "Since he's not doing it anymore. He told me he can't get any more under-the-counter stuff."

Elizabeth met her worried gaze. "Now that Kenny is no longer alive to supply him."

"That doesn't mean he killed him."

"But he may know who did."

"Oh, crikey," Violet whispered.

Elizabeth let out her breath. "Try not to worry. I'll talk to him tomorrow and let's hope we are jumping to conclusions."

She changed the subject then, determined not to dwell on the subject until she'd had a chance to talk with Percy. But her heart was heavy with worry when she retired that night. She hated to think that someone living in the peaceful village of Sitting Marsh could be responsible for the violent death of an American airman. Apparently all in the name of greed.

CHAPTER

❀ 13 ❀

The following day Elizabeth rode her motorcycle into town, hoping to avoid the early-morning rush of shoppers. Much to her relief, only three customers remained in the grocer's shop when she arrived there. Unfortunately, one of them happened to be Rita Crumm.

Percy greeted Elizabeth when she walked in, then went back to stacking cans of soup on the shelves.

Flanked by two of her regular cronies, Marge and Florrie, Rita stood at the bacon counter and gave Elizabeth a derogatory smile. "Something wrong with Violet, your ladyship?" she inquired, her booming voice loud enough to be heard halfway down the street.

Elizabeth frowned. "Violet? Not as far as I know. She seemed perfectly healthy when she served up breakfast this morning."

Rita peered down her nose. She was an unusually tall woman, which gave her a definite advantage when attempting to look haughty. Since she deemed everyone in the village beneath her consideration, and that included the lady of the manor, she spent a good deal of her time attempting to look haughty.

"Well," she said, with what Elizabeth considered a somewhat vulgar sniff, "I was just wondering, since this is the second time you've been in this shop and you don't usually do your own shopping."

The envy in her voice was obvious. Elizabeth was quite aware that Rita would give up her only daughter if it meant having a housekeeper. The fact that Lily Crumm was every bit as objectionable as her mother would prove her no great loss in Elizabeth's opinion. "And I'm not doing any shopping now," she informed Rita. "This is purely a social visit. I assume you have no objection to that?"

Having had the wind taken out of her sails, so to speak, Rita's eyes glittered. "It's not my place to object, Lady Elizabeth. I was simply commenting on the rare occasion one sees you inside a shop. I was concerned about Violet's health, that's all."

"How very kind of you." Elizabeth smiled sweetly at her. "I'll be certain to pass on your concern. I'm quite sure Violet will be as flabbergasted as I am."

Rita tossed her head, but apparently decided to ignore the barb. "I expect you'd like to know that the pavilion has been thoroughly spring-cleaned, your ladyship. It's sparkling. You won't even recognize it."

"Well, thank you so much, ladies." Elizabeth beamed at Florrie and Marge, both of whom glanced at Rita before murmuring almost in unison, "Pleasure, your ladyship."

"We shall all be in attendance this evening to watch the cricket lesson," Rita announced, much to Elizabeth's dismay.

She tried to sound indifferent when she answered, "Oh, really? I shouldn't think it would be too exciting."

"Whenever there are Yanks around," Florrie said with a lecherous wink, "there's always some excitement."

"Shut up, Florrie," Rita said rudely. "We're not there to gape at the Yanks. We're taking refreshments down there for them. Lemonade and cream soda."

"If you ask me, them Yanks would much rather have a glass of beer," Marge said daringly.

"Well, if they want beer, they'll have to blinking bring it themselves." Rita coughed. "If you'll excuse my French, m'm."

"You're excused," Elizabeth said cheerfully. "But really, there's no need to make a fuss. We'll simply be trying to teach the Americans how to play the game, that's all. They won't actually play until the match on Wednesday."

"I don't know how much they'll learn in an hour or two, m'm," Percy put in from the back of the shop. "Not much time to teach someone the finer points of the game."

"I don't think they are expecting to become experts at it, Percy." Elizabeth smiled at him. "Just do your best. I'm sure the Americans will be grateful for any pointers you can give them."

"Well," Rita announced, her tone clearly indicating that she'd become bored with the conversation, "I can't stand around and chatter like this all day. I have more important things to do. Good day to you, Lady Elizabeth. We will see you tonight at the cricket field."

Not if I can help it, Elizabeth thought grimly. She watched Rita sweep out of the shop, followed dutifully by her two unwilling handmaidens.

Percy shook his head and came toward her. "Don't pay them any attention, your ladyship. Bored, that's what they are. Do them all good to get a job at the factory. I hear they're begging for help down there."

Elizabeth laughed. "Somehow I can't imagine Rita wrapping her head in a scarf and clambering over an airplane wielding a blowtorch. She'd terrorize everyone around her."

"Likely she would at that, m'm." Percy joined in her laughter, then wiped his hands on his apron. "So what can I do for you today, your ladyship? If you came to ask me if I'll be at the cricket lesson, I wouldn't miss it. Love the game meself, though I haven't played in a good many years."

"Actually, I was wondering if you'd care to help umpire the match on Wednesday. Captain Carbunkle has offered his services as well, though his attention span can be somewhat limited. I'd appreciate it if you could spare the time?"

Percy looked surprised, but nodded eagerly. "Love to, m'm. Wednesday is half-closing, so there won't be no problem. I'll have to brush up on the old laws a bit, but that won't take long. You can count on me."

"Thank you, Percy. I knew you wouldn't let me down." Now that the time had come to question him about the black market trade, she was suddenly at a loss for words. What if he had been Kenny's contact? If so, then he could well have killed the man. It was very unlikely that he would tell her so, but if he couldn't deny it to her satisfaction, then she would be honor bound to go to the authorities and tell them what she knew.

She wished now that she had left well alone, and let the American investigators solve the case. But then Earl had asked for her help, and she had promised to see what she could do. She owed it to him to see this through, even if it meant betraying a trusted friend and resident of Sitting Marsh. How she hated the thought of that.

Taking a deep breath, she braced herself for the worst. "Percy, there's something I need to talk to you about."

His smile vanished immediately, to be replaced by a wary frown. "Sounds serious, your ladyship. Nothing I've done, I hope?"

"Well, that's what I need you to tell me." Elizabeth

glanced apprehensively at the door, but now that it was the lunch hour, the main street was practically deserted.

Percy stared at her for several seconds. "Well, perhaps it is time we had a little talk," he said finally.

She watched him walk over to the door and close it. A prickling feeling touched her spine when he also twisted the key in the lock, and swung the OPEN notice around to CLOSED. "Now we won't be disturbed, m'm," he added quietly.

Heart pounding uncomfortably, Elizabeth watched him walk behind the counter. "I won't keep you a minute, Percy," she said hurriedly. "There's no need to lock the door."

"Oh, I always lock it at lunchtime, m'm." Percy picked up a large carving knife and ran his thumb slowly down the razor-sharp blade. "Gives me some time to meself, you see."

Something cold slithered down Elizabeth's back. Her lips felt quite dry when she said faintly, "Maybe this isn't a good time after all. Why don't we talk tonight at the cricket field. I have several errands to run—"

"No, your ladyship. Now is the right time." Sunlight glinted on the wicked blade as Percy raised the knife to his shoulder.

With a measuring glance at the door, she backed carefully away from the counter.

The vicious-looking weapon hovered in the air, then with a swift, savage thrust, Percy slammed the lethal blade down. It hit the board with a sickening thud.

Elizabeth's hand flew to her mouth as she uttered a frightened little squeak.

Percy looked up with a smile. "Care for a slice of Gorgonzola, your ladyship? Off the ration, of course. Just don't tell anyone." With a wink he held out a chunk of the blue-veined cheese.

Feeling foolish, Elizabeth took the offering with a trembling hand and bit off a small piece. Her heart still thumped uneasily against her ribs, and she had difficulty swallowing the tangy-tasting morsel. By the time she had finally choked it down, Percy had laid down the knife.

He took a bite out of the chunk of cheese in his hand, then came around the counter. "Here," he said, offering her a couple of water biscuits, "these will go down good with it."

"Thank you." She coughed, cleared her throat, and took the biscuits from him. "Actually, it was the rationing thing I rather wanted to talk to you about."

Percy's eyebrows raised, his expression one of pure innocence. "Rationing, m'm?"

Elizabeth nodded. There was no point in beating about the bush now. She had to finish what she'd started. "It's come—" She broke off, appalled to hear the overly high-pitched note in her voice. Once more she cleared her throat, and tried again. "It has come to my attention, Percy, that you may have been supplying certain members of this community with under-the-counter goods."

Her shattered nerves had made her sound overly stern, and Percy frowned. "Who told you that, m'm?"

"It really doesn't matter who told me, does it. Just tell me if it's true or not."

For a long moment he stared at her, his mental battle with his conscience causing one eyelid to twitch uncontrollably. Then he uttered a long sigh. "All right. I'm really sorry, m'm. Truly I am. Yes, I was handing out some stuff for a while. Not doing it anymore, though. I know it was wrong, but I just wanted to help people out, that's all. There wasn't anything in it for me, honest. I paid through the nose for it. But I got tired of having to say no so many times when the ladies kept asking for a little extra on the scales. You know how it is, your lady-ship. It's wartime. You have to look out for people, don't you."

Elizabeth gulped. Without realizing, she'd finished the

entire piece of cheese while he was talking. She hadn't tasted one bit of it. "I do know exactly what you mean, Percy."

"Yeah, well, the government keeps a stern eye on blokes like us. We have to account for everything that goes out of here, and if we're short on the coupons, well, then we get shorted the next month and we have to make up for it. So, when I saw the chance to give everyone a little bit of a treat, I couldn't turn it down, now, could I, m'm?"

"Of course not, Percy." She had to stop agreeing with everything he said, she thought desperately.

"Well then, we're all right, then, are we?"

"Not exactly." Her fingers still shook as she brushed crumbs from her wool jacket. "There's the little matter of Kenny Morris's murder."

Percy's eyebrows almost disappeared into his hairline. "Murder? What's that got to do with anything?"

Feeling only a tad reassured, she explained, "Kenny Morris was supplying stolen goods from the base. I assume he's the one from whom you obtained your little treats."

"Oh, my." Percy's face was ashen. He clutched his chest and grabbed the counter for support. "Oh, good God. I'm in trouble, aren't I?"

"You could quite well be." Now she was beginning to feel a bit sorry for the poor man. "After all, Kenny Morris is dead, and you had underhanded dealings with him . . ."

"No, m'm, I didn't."

". . . so naturally one would . . . I beg your pardon?"

"I didn't have no underhanded nothing with Kenny Morris. I never even met the man. I swear it."

Hope definitely on the rise, Elizabeth prompted, "So how did you get the goods? Someone else delivered them?"

Percy closed his eyes for a moment, then walked back

behind the counter. He picked up a kitchen towel and began wiping his hands on it. His face was still pale, and she noticed his hands trembled as he put down the towel. "Look, I don't want to get no one into trouble, especially a nice little old lady like Henrietta Jones, but I've got to look out for myself here, haven't I. I could be in big trouble. After all, we're talking about a murder here."

Elizabeth frowned. "What does Henrietta Jones have to do with anything?"

Percy shrugged. "Well, she was the one that supplied me with the stuff, wasn't she."

Elizabeth felt her jaw go slack. "Henrietta Jones?"

"That's right, your ladyship. Henrietta Jones."

"Henrietta *Jones*?" Elizabeth repeated. Thoroughly confused, she tried to make sense of this latest development. "I don't understand. How could she be your supplier? She doesn't drive a vehicle. She told me so."

Percy tucked his thumbs into the bib of his apron. "She didn't deliver it. She let me know when she had something and I went out there and picked it up. One case at a time. Sometimes I'd bring her back with me so she could shop in town, then I'd run her back home. Least I could do, really. Though I paid her bloody well for the goods."

"But where on earth did she get stolen goods?" Elizabeth demanded, still unable to accept what she was hearing.

"Her grandson, Charlie. He lives in London, you see. Now and again he comes down to check up on her, and he was bringing a case or two of food with him. He works at some American distribution center in the city. Mind you, I don't know if the stuff was stolen or not. He told the old lady he was buying the surplus cheap. Though if you ask me, I reckon he copped a case or two when no one was looking."

This time only one of Elizabeth's eyebrows lifted.

Percy shrugged. "Well, they all do it, m'm, don't they. Besides, can't really blame him when he's only trying to help the old lady out."

"Indeed." Elizabeth shook her head in disbelief. "Henrietta Jones. But why would she sell the supplies to you if they were a gift from her grandson?"

"Couldn't eat it all, m'm, could she. A case of peaches goes a long way. Besides, I reckon she could use the money."

"It sounds as if she had a nice little business going on there."

"Well, she won't get no more for a while now. Charlie told his grandmother he couldn't get no more extra rations for a while. I reckon he got caught, and that put a stop to it."

"I see." Her head was beginning to ache. She needed time to think about everything she'd heard. "There's just one more thing." She pointed to the display counter. "Where did you get that strange-looking straw? I've never seen green straw before."

"Ah, that's American, that's why. Came in those crates I bought from Henrietta. Looks really nice in my counter, though it's not real straw. Made of paper, it is. Looks real, though, doesn't it?"

"It certainly does," Elizabeth said thoughtfully. "Well, I'll be getting along then, Percy. Thank you for telling me everything. We'll see you tonight at the cricket field then?"

Percy hurried around the counter. "Let me get the door for you, your ladyship." He waited until she was about to step out into the street before adding anxiously, "So what's going to happen now? Am I in trouble over this?"

Elizabeth smiled at him. "I hope not, Percy, though I'd be very careful before accepting stolen goods in the future."

"Oh, I will, m'm. That's a promise. I didn't have nothing to do with that murder, that I swear."

"Try not to worry about it." She gave him a graceful wave of her hand and headed for her motorcycle.

On the ride home she went over everything in her mind. The paper straw in the cricket pavilion matched the straw in Percy's display counter. Straw that the American military used in crates. Crates that were sent to the bases. Kenny must have been delivering those crates to the pavilion, which would explain the huge tire wheels. Whoever had bought them had stored them there until he could get rid of them.

Until word got out of the upcoming cricket match, in which case the contact would have had to find another place to store the supplies.

He'd moved out the crates, leaving pieces of the packing behind—the same packing that Percy had used in his display. The packing he said he got out of the crates he bought from Henrietta.

Percy, of course, could be lying. Though it would take some imagination to make up a story like that. But then, if he was telling the truth, it would appear that Henrietta's grandson could have been Kenny Morris's contact. Or at least one of them. In which case, he could also be the murderer.

Elizabeth's heart ached for the elderly woman. She could only hope that she was wrong about all this, for if she proved to be right, Henrietta Jones was facing a terrible heartbreak.

She thought about paying the widow a visit that afternoon, then decided against it. She needed more time to sort things out in her mind before she upset the frail old woman. Besides, she had a lot to do before the cricket lesson this evening. Henrietta would just have to wait until tomorrow.

CHAPTER
❈ 14 ❈

Rita Crumm had been right, for once. Elizabeth hardly recognized the pavilion when she walked into the main hall later that afternoon. Windows gleamed and the floors had been scrubbed almost white. Long trestle tables, borrowed from the town hall no doubt, lined the walls, their bright pink paper tablecloths reaching to the floor.

Rita and her crew had even hung a few garlands of twisted red, white, and blue crepe paper from the low-lying beams, and someone had donated a dilapidated dartboard to hang on the wall.

The whole place looked quite festive, and Elizabeth had to acknowledge that Rita and her Housewives League had done themselves proud.

Even Violet, who never had a good word to say about any member of Rita's entourage, muttered something that might have passed for a compliment under her breath.

Percy arrived early, decked out in white trousers, white shirt, and the obligatory white sleeveless sweater with bands of blue at the neck and armholes.

"Blimey," Violet muttered, "doesn't he look spiffy all of a sudden. Thought this was just a practice run. Hope he don't get that lot dirty before Wednesday."

Elizabeth was spared from answering her when a loud popping, banging, and wheezing signaled the arrival of Captain Carbunkle in his silver 1934 MG, which had somehow survived years of the captain's erratic and sometimes suicidal driving.

Following on his heels came a waving, wobbling line of women on bicycles, headed up by the inimitable Rita Crumm. Shortly after they'd dismounted, the bus arrived and spilled out a host of villagers all anxious to watch the Yanks attempt to learn one of Great Britain's national pastimes—the honorable game of cricket.

The pavilion quickly filled up with people, all seemingly talking at once. Elizabeth spied Polly briefly in the crowd, but right then a commotion out front indicated that the noisy engines she heard were jeeps pulling up at the entrance.

Violet was deep in an animated conversation with Bessie, and Elizabeth drifted over to the door, telling herself that she really needed to count heads if she were to organize the lesson.

Reaching the top of the steps, she squinted across the car park where American airmen were scrambling out of the jeeps. There seemed to be quite a few more than eleven would-be players. No doubt some of them were eager onlookers.

A shriek to her right caught her attention, just in time to see Polly fling herself into the open arms of Sam Cutter. The officer swung the young girl off her feet, and she clung to his neck, her cheeks glowing.

Elizabeth envied her secretary right then. How liberating it must be not to worry about convention or what other people thought. She turned back to the car park, her heart sinking when she failed to see the tall figure of Earl Monroe striding toward her.

It didn't mean anything had happened to him, she assured herself, trying not to remember the tense expression on his face that morning. He was simply held up at the base, that was all. Though whatever it was that delayed him had to be critical for him to miss the lesson, since he was captaining the team.

In an attempt to stem the panic that threatened to rise, she hurried over to Sam Cutter, who stood with his arms around Polly, looking at her as if he couldn't bear to let her go.

Again Elizabeth had to stifle a wave of envy. Whatever had happened to her resolve to remain indifferent to the male species? Surely she could not be succumbing to the general attitude to make every moment count and to blazes with what tomorrow might bring?

She knew better than that. The hard lessons she'd learned through her own disastrous marriage had taught her well. Yet these days she was in constant danger of forgetting all that she had suffered and lost. It would be a bad mistake to allow that to happen. Especially when it came to a certain married major in the United States Army Air Force.

Polly caught sight of her first when she approached, and hastily stepped out of the circle of Sam Cutter's arms. He turned to see the cause of Polly's embarrassment, and gave Elizabeth a beaming smile.

"Hi, your ladyship! Good to see you again."

"Thank you, Squadron Leader. I was very pleased to hear that you had been released from the base." She glanced at Polly, whose face was now a bright pink. "I'm sure my secretary is even more happy."

"Yes, ma'am." Sam grinned, while Polly looked uncomfortable.

As well she should, Elizabeth thought wryly. She couldn't help wondering if Sam was aware of Polly's tender age, then decided it was none of her business. In these uncertain days problems such as being too young or too old didn't seem to have much significance.

"We've been looking forward to learning how to play cricket, ma'am," Sam said, nodding his head out to midfield.

"Yes, well, I hope the men have managed to round up enough cricket bats and balls for the big game." Elizabeth was aching to ask if Earl would be there for the lesson. She was trying to think of a way to phrase the question when directly behind her his deep voice spoke in his familiar drawl.

"Hi there. Sorry I'm late."

It took a tremendous amount of discipline not to let the joy shine in her face. She turned to look at him, struggling to hide the sheer pleasure she felt as she met his warm gaze. "Major Monroe! How nice to see you again. I'm so glad you could be with us this evening."

"Lady Elizabeth. I'm real happy to be here." He reached for her hand, and completely floored her by raising her fingers to his lips.

Polly made a soft sound in her throat, while Elizabeth stood transfixed. She felt as if the entire world had suddenly rocked to a full stop.

The beautiful moment was broken by a strident voice bellowing to be heard above everyone else. "If we don't get this bloody lesson started, it'll be bleeding dark before anyone's hit the flippin' ball."

Elizabeth winced, and Polly giggled. "That's Rita getting on her high horse," she said, reaching for Sam's hand. "Come on, let's get out there and show them what the Yanks can do with a cricket ball."

"Guess I'd better join them," Earl said, as the men

streamed onto the field. "The team's not going to play too well if their captain hasn't a clue what he's doing."

"Quite right." Elizabeth finally found her composure. "You'd better get going, then."

He looked as if he wanted to say something important, then apparently changed his mind, and grinned instead. "Aren't you supposed to give me a scarf or something to wear?"

She shook her head. "That's jousting. The knight tied his lady's scarf onto his lance. One of those frothy silk things. Somehow tying a woolly scarf to a cricket bat doesn't have the same aura of romance to it."

"Too bad. Here." He pulled off his cap and handed it to her. "You can hold this for me instead."

Before she could answer, he smoothed a hand over his hair, then strode off across the field to join his team-mates.

The next hour, as Elizabeth commented later, could only be described as pure bedlam. The Americans, used to playing baseball, had the devil of a job trying to hold the long, narrow cricket bat in the right position, much less actually hit the ball.

Captain Carbunkle spent several long-winded minutes explaining the concept of trying to prevent the bails from leaving the wickets, and how to score runs. Then the first volunteer, a beefy American with ginger hair, stepped up to the wicket, hefted the bat and waited for Percy to bowl.

Percy took his run and the ball came in low and fast. Taken by surprise, the American lifted the bat and wielded it as if he were attempting to hit a baseball. Realizing at the last minute that the ball was lower than he expected, he swung the bat behind him and knocked the bails flying.

"You're out!" Carbunkle bellowed.

He was a big man, with a full beard and a voice like

a foghorn. The American leaped in the air and dropped the bat. "Whaddaya mean, I'm out?"

"Bails off the wickets." Carbunkle held up the small pieces of rounded wood that had rested on the three wooden stumps. "That means you're out."

"What about my three strikes?"

Carbunkle looked confused. "Don't know anything about strikes, young fella. All I can tell you is you're out, until the next over, that is. Then you'll be in again."

The American scratched his head. "What's over? I haven't even begun to play yet."

"Nothing's over yet. But you're out for this over, and you can't come in again until this over is over and the next over begins."

Giving up, the American ambled off the field shaking his head, amidst raucous comments from the audience. Rita's voice, naturally, was the loudest. "Thought you Yanks could do everything!" she yelled, amidst giggles from her stalwart companions.

The next striker up, a short, skinny young man with a fierce, intent frown, appeared to hold the bat correctly, but at the last minute took a couple of steps forward and the ball glanced off his arm.

"LBW!" Carbunkle shouted gleefully.

"What the heck is that?" the young American demanded.

"Leg before wicket, sir. You're out."

"My legs have to be in front of the wicket or I can't hit the damn ball."

"No, sir, the ball hit you before you hit it, so it's leg before wicket."

"It didn't hit my leg, it hit my friggin' arm!"

"It doesn't have to hit your leg, laddie. It just has to hit anywhere on your body."

"Then why is it called leg before wicket?"

"Search me. It's in the laws, isn't it."

Another disgusted player walked off the field to be greeted by more catcalls.

And so it went on. Finally, after an hour and a half of bellowing, explaining, complaining, and jeering, the exhausted coaches had to acknowledge one thing. The Yanks didn't stand a hope in hell of winning the cricket match on Wednesday.

The next morning Elizabeth rode her motorcycle back through town and out on the coast road to visit Henrietta Jones. It was a pleasant ride, with just enough breeze to fan her face as she swopped down the hill and around the long curve.

She had securely fastened a plaid wool scarf around her head, and today she wore goggles to protect her eyes. Normally she rode without them, claiming she could see better without the restricting frames. Lately, however, the cold wind had caused her eyes to water quite profusely, thus impairing her vision more so than wearing the goggles.

Henrietta must have been seated in the window, since she answered Elizabeth's loud rapping of the door knocker. Elizabeth had to wonder how many visitors the elderly widow missed by failing to hear them at her door. Then again, by all accounts, Henrietta didn't have that many visitors.

The old lady seemed surprised to see her, but invited her in with a wide sweep of her arm. "So nice of you to call on me," she said in her gravelly voice, as Elizabeth followed her into the cottage. The living room smelled as if a dozen dogs lived in there. Obviously Charlie's care-giving didn't extend to housework.

"Can I get you some tea and crumpets?" Henrietta motioned to the threadbare settee, and Elizabeth lowered herself gingerly onto the sagging springs.

This time she'd armed herself with a small blackboard and chalk. *Thank you, no,* she wrote hastily, the vision

of the dogs still with her. She showed the blackboard to
Henrietta, who adjusted her glasses and peered at the
words, nodding her understanding.

After scrubbing out the letters with her eraser, Elizabeth wrote, *Just wanted to see how you were doing. Do
you need a ride into town?* Now that Percy wouldn't be
calling on her, the old lady would need someone else to
take her shopping.

Henrietta shook her head. "No, thank you, Lady Elizabeth. As a matter of fact, I've been thinking about leaving Sitting Marsh and going back to London to live."

"Really!" Elizabeth regarded her with open curiosity,
then wrote, *Aren't you worried about the bombing?*

Henrietta shook her head, and a stray hair or two
floated to the floor. "Not really. At my age one doesn't
worry about things like that. I'll go when my number's
up, no matter where I am. Just like everyone else."

Elizabeth shivered, unable to prevent the spasm of
pain at the thought of her parents perishing in the lethal
blast of a German bomb. Quickly she scribbled, *What
does your grandson think about you going back to the
city?*

Henrietta shrugged. "Oh, he's happy about it. Save
him coming down. Getting a bit tired of that, he was.
Can't blame him, really. It's not much fun taking care
of an old lady. This way I'll be a lot closer so he can
keep an eye on me. Good boy, that, our Charlie."

Elizabeth nodded, her anxiety mounting. If Charlie
was involved in Kenny's murder, then the poor old lady
would have no one to take care of her in London.
Whereas if she stayed in Sitting Marsh, she'd at least
have a couple of people calling in on her now and again
to make sure she was all right.

Intent now on finding out what she could about Charlie's whereabouts that night, she wrote, *How often does
Charlie get down here? Every weekend?*

"Oh, no, not every weekend, no." Henrietta awkwardly pulled a cushion out from behind her, plumped it up, and stuffed it behind her back again. Elizabeth could tell from the way the old lady moved that her rheumatism was bothering her again. She felt an aching sympathy for the poor woman. It was so sad to see someone alone and in pain much of the time with only a wayward grandson to care about her.

So when was the last time he was down? she persisted. *Last weekend? The weekend before?*

Henrietta squinted her eyes as if she were trying to remember. "Not last weekend, for sure. And the weekend before that, he was in London at my cousin's funeral. So he didn't come down then, neither."

He spent the entire weekend at the funeral?

Henrietta peered at her as if wondering why she was being questioned so thoroughly.

Trying to look indifferent, Elizabeth wrote, *You surprised me. Funerals don't usually last all weekend.*

"They do if you're Irish Catholic," Henrietta said dryly. "You know the Irish. Any excuse to drink. The wake went on all day and night. Funeral was on Saturday and they didn't give up drinking and eating until Sunday night." She uttered what sounded very much like a snort. "Never seen anything like it in all my born days."

Elizabeth looked at her in surprise, then wrote, *You were there?*

Henrietta tapped the arm of her chair with her thick fingers. "I was there, yes. Thanks to our Charlie. He came down on the Friday to get me, and brought me home on Monday. Took time off work to do that, he did. Like I said, good boy, that Charlie."

You were with him the entire weekend?

"Stayed right in his flat, I did. Gave me his own bed, while he slept on the sofa. Never left me side the whole weekend."

Elizabeth managed a weak smile and scribbled, *Nice of him. You must have enjoyed that.*

"I did." Henrietta nodded vigorously. "In fact, I enjoyed it so much, that's when I decided I might as well go back to London to stay."

So when do you plan on leaving? Elizabeth glanced at the clock on the mantelpiece. It's loud tick was somewhat distracting. Not that Henrietta would be bothered by it, of course.

"Just as soon as Charlie can get down here and help me pack." Henrietta followed Elizabeth's glance. "Don't let me keep you, Lady Elizabeth. I'm sure you have better things to do than spend time gossiping with me."

Grateful for the cue, Elizabeth rose. *Let me know when you plan to leave,* she wrote on the slate.

Henrietta smiled. "You'll be the first to know, Lady Elizabeth. Other than Charlie, that is."

Elizabeth returned the smile and quickly left. Not that she felt like smiling. Yet another closed trail. How she hated all these dead ends. It wasn't just for Earl now, that she wanted to find out what happened. Or for Sam Cutter, or Polly.

She hated to admit defeat. Somewhere, somehow along the line she had the niggling feeling that she knew something important. Something that could possibly shed light on the mystery. She'd had that feeling before, the certainty that something crucial was floating in her mind just beyond reach. All she had to do was trap it and hold it down long enough to examine it.

No matter how intensely she tried, however, she couldn't think what it could be that she knew and didn't know she knew. It was too vague, too deep in her subconscious mind. She would simply have to wait and hope that it surfaced sometime soon. Because although she wasn't quite sure why, she felt a certain sense of urgency, as if time were running out. And that was the most unsettling notion of all.

• • •

The day of the cricket match dawned with a layer of heavy white clouds drifting across the pale blue sky. Watching them anxiously from time to time, Elizabeth was relieved to see the minute patches of blue gradually spread out, and by noon the skies had cleared and a warm sun prevailed upon the players assembled at the cricket field.

The American jeeps had pulled up on one side of the car park when she arrived and the British army lorries were lined up on the other. Inside the pavilion, Rita's housewives bustled around, preparing the tables for the big feast. The army captain in charge of the soldiers had volunteered to fetch the food from Bessie's bakery after the match, therefore eliminating the worry of keeping everything fresh all afternoon.

In spite of a distinct chill from a brisk ocean breeze, deck chairs filled with onlookers, mostly women, sat in front of the pavilion balcony with a full view of the field.

Although the players looked somewhat out of sorts dressed in army trousers and undershirts, the excitement and tension far surpassed the usual games of cricket that had been played there before the war.

Desmond had done a remarkable job of rolling and smoothing the pitch and defining the creases, and Elizabeth was looking forward to watching the match.

She barely had time to speak to Earl before the umpires called the first players in. Making up her mind to have a chat with him later, she settled down to enjoy the game.

It soon became quite apparent that the Americans were outmatched. The British soldiers piled up the runs, and it was fairly obvious to everyone there that they thoroughly enjoyed their triumph over their rivals.

Now and again a rather crude remark from the British soldiers drifted across the field, but for the most part the Americans either didn't understand the phrase or chose to ignore it. All in all, considering the vast inequity in the skills of the players, the whole game was quite civilized.

When the victorious team finally walked off the field, the crowing over their opponents was quite good-natured, with the Americans promising a very different outcome with the return match of baseball.

Much to Elizabeth's delight, and Violet's disbelief, the feast also progressed without incident, no doubt because Rita and her housewives went out of their way to make a fuss of the British soldiers, leaving the Americans to the village girls, for which they were no doubt divinely grateful.

Elizabeth felt the entire event was a rousing success, and felt inordinately pleased with herself. Now, if only the baseball game turned out half as well, it could mean she had made great strides in her quest to unite the British and the Americans in Sitting Marsh.

CHAPTER

❀ 15 ❀

Later, while discussing the game over a glass of sherry in the conservatory, she congratulated Earl on the exemplary conduct of his team.

"They all behaved like perfect gentlemen," she told him, neglecting to confess she saw most of the Americans sneak out of the pavilion with a village girl in tow before the feast was over.

"They knew they were outclassed." Earl grinned at her. "Bad as the New York Yankees losing to the Cardinals in the World Series this year. Weird game, though. I don't think anyone on my team understood the rules."

"Don't let that bother you. Most of the British don't understand them, either." Elizabeth stretched her feet out in front of her. She sat in her usual spot on the wicker divan, while Earl rocked gently to and fro on the rocking chair.

"Actually," she added, when he didn't answer, "as a rule I find the game quite boring. I must admit, this afternoon's contest was quite invigorating for a change."

"I had a good time. Made a change from the touch football we play on the base."

She hated to put a dampener on the pleasant conversation, but she felt compelled to tell him what had transpired over the past couple of days. After relating her conversation with Percy, she told him how she'd suspected Henrietta's grandson of being Kenny's contact. "After talking to her, though, I'm convinced he wasn't involved. It was just coincidence that he brought supplies down for Henrietta at the same time Kenny was dealing with his own stolen goods."

"Ironic when you think about it," Earl observed. "If this Charlie had known about Kenny Morris, he wouldn't have had to bring the stuff all the way down from London. He could have bought it from Kenny and saved himself the trouble."

"Except that Charlie wasn't interested in buying anything," Elizabeth reminded him. "Charlie was stealing from the distribution center where he worked."

"An American PX, you mean."

She stared at him. "I really don't know. Though . . . yes . . . it must have been, because Henrietta had some of those biscuits with little pieces of chocolate in them."

"Chocolate chip cookies," Earl said, looking amused.

"Is that what they're called? How droll! Anyway, if she had American biscuits—"

"Cookies."

"Whatever. Then Charlie had to be stealing from an American establishment."

"The coincidence gets thicker."

"It does, indeed." Her mind worked at the problem. "It had to be coincidence, though. Henrietta was quite positive about the weekend she spent with Charlie in London. The same weekend of the murder."

"You don't think she could be lying, to protect her grandson?"

"I don't know." She thought about it. "But I don't think so. She's such a straitlaced little old lady. I don't think she'd take any nonsense from her grandson. She thinks the world of him. I don't think she has an inkling that Charlie stole that stuff. That's if he did steal it. He could have been telling the truth about buying surplus."

"If he did, then someone had to steal it in the first place. The American military doesn't sell supplies to civilians."

"I suppose not. In any case, it's all a moot point. I'm no closer to solving the mystery than your investigators. Charlie is the only person on the list of suspects who has an alibi. The others—Percy Bodkins, Brian Forrester, and, as much as you don't want to hear this, Sam Cutter—all had possible motives and no real alibi. Any one of them could be lying. But which one? And how do we prove it?"

"Good question." Earl reached for his glass and drained it. "The answer is, we don't. We stop worrying about it and let the investigators do their job."

Elizabeth frowned. "It isn't that easy to forget it. That young man was strangled to death in the bell tower of Sitting Marsh. I owe it to his grieving parents, as well as the villagers, to find out who has done this. I can't rest knowing that a murderer is still lurking around, congratulating himself on getting away with a despicable crime."

Earl stopped rocking the chair. "Elizabeth, you've done the best you possibly could to solve this murder. That's all anyone can do. I don't like the thought of you poking around in something that could be dangerous. So, please, do me a favor and just forget about it."

As always, when he used her first name, the pleasurable afterglow chased everything else from her mind. "When do you think you can arrange the baseball match?" she asked, after a moment of companionable silence.

He grinned. "Glutton for punishment, you English."

"Not at all. We might just beat you at your own game."

"You can always dream, I guess."

Elizabeth pursed her lips. "It wouldn't be the first time that overconfidence bred disaster."

"If there's one thing us Yanks have going for us, it's our overwhelming confidence."

"So I noticed."

"It's got us through a few tight spots in the past."

Sobered by the comment, she said quietly, "I pray to God it gets you through the rest of them."

His gaze rested on her face for a moment before he answered. "I reckon we could all use the prayers."

He continued to hold her gaze until she felt quite breathless. She wanted to say something—anything, but was afraid that whatever she said would betray the rapid beat of her heart.

She was quite relieved when he said abruptly, "Where are George and Gracie?"

"In the kitchen with Violet. Lying by the fire, no doubt."

"I'll get busy with that fence in the stables in a day or two."

She thought about that for several seconds before saying, "I just don't feel comfortable about putting them out in the stables. I'm sorry, Earl, I know you said they are outdoor dogs, and I promise I'll get them outside as often as necessary, but I really don't think they consider themselves to be outdoor dogs and I just think they are too young and it would be too upsetting for them—"

His raised hand halted her rush of words. "Whoa, easy there. I never said they couldn't live in the house. I thought you were having problems with that, so I suggested the stables. If you want them in the house, then by all means keep them here. It's your call."

She felt ridiculous, knowing that her small outburst was due more to her chaotic emotions than concern about the puppies. "Of course. And I think I shall keep them in the house. For now, anyway."

"Good for you." He raised an eyebrow. "Is Violet giving you a bad time about the dogs?"

"What? Oh, no, not really. Violet complains about everything, and as for Martin, he forgets what he's complaining about the minute he starts talking."

"Yeah, I noticed he's a little slow on the uptake. Not surprising, considering his age."

"I know." She looked down at her hands. "I worry about him at times. He seems to get more vague and confused as the weeks go by." She told him about the unlucky tourist Martin had mistakenly apprehended as an intruder.

Earl laughed. "At least he's still trying to protect you."

"I know." She smiled with him. "Sweet, isn't it."

"Very."

"Especially since I'm the one who should be protecting him."

"You make a great mother hen."

"Is that supposed to be a compliment?"

"You bet it is. I can't think of any woman I'd want more in my corner if my back was to the wall."

His comment pleased her immensely. She actually felt her cheeks warming, something that didn't happen too often.

"Well, I'd better get back to my quarters. I still have some paperwork to do." Earl rose, and reluctantly, she bid him good night.

"You will let me know about the baseball game?" she reminded him as she showed him out the door.

"You bet. Just as soon as I can get something arranged."

She had to be content with that.

After he left, she went back to the divan to finish her sherry. She sat for a long time mulling over what she knew about that fateful night Kenny Morris had died.

It did seem rather a coincidence that Charlie had been bringing down American supplies for his grandmother at the same time Kenny Morris had been dealing in the same thing.

What if Charlie had lied to Henrietta about where he got the goods? What if he'd got them from Kenny when he arrived in Sitting Marsh instead? That would make a lot more sense.

But if Charlie was buying only a case at a time, why would Kenny need a large truck to transport the goods? He could have simply thrown it in a jeep. Unless there were more than one contact involved in the black market business.

Elizabeth sat up straight, nearly spilling her sherry. Kenny was storing supplies in the pavilion, until he'd heard about the cricket match. Kenny would have had to find another storage place. Somewhere nearby.

There weren't that many places where someone could hide a truckload of goods. The crates could still be somewhere in the village. If she could find those goods, or at least traces of where they'd been stored, it might give her a clue that could help lead to Kenny's killer.

All she had to do was look for them.

The next morning Elizabeth cleaned out her beige handbag. Now that autumn had descended upon the countryside, the time for wearing beige shoes and bag had definitely passed.

After tipping everything out of the bag onto her bed, she fetched her black winter handbag and started sorting through the jumble scattered over the eiderdown.

She found the usual assortment of safety pins, hair pins, lipstick, box of aspirin, comb, keys, and the torn half of a raffle ticket, as well as a creased photograph of herself with her parents when she was six.

She also found the silver comb, which, until now, she'd completely forgotten about. Staring at it, she envisioned Henrietta, shaking her head and dislodging gray hairs that floated to the floor.

Of course. Why hadn't she thought to ask her? True, the vicar had mentioned the comb to his parishioners, but if he'd announced it from the pulpit, Henrietta would have been unable to hear him.

Elizabeth slipped the comb into her handbag. She planned on taking a ride around the village that morning in the hopes of spotting somewhere that could be used for storing a load of crates. She would drop in to see Henrietta first, she decided, and ask her if she was the owner of the comb.

As it happened, Henrietta was in her garden when Elizabeth arrived there a little later. She stood at the door of the garden shed, apparently absorbed in its contents. She gave no sign of having heard the roar of Elizabeth's motorcycle, but remained motionless as Elizabeth walked down the path toward her.

She finally had to tap the elderly lady on the shoulder to get her attention.

Henrietta spun around, closing the door of the shed as she did so. "Oh, Lady Elizabeth," she cried, clutching her throat, "you quite startled me."

It wasn't until that moment that Elizabeth remembered she hadn't brought the blackboard. Hoping she wouldn't need it, she rummaged in her handbag until she found the comb.

Holding it out to Henrietta she said loudly, "Does this belong to you?"

Henrietta's pale blue eyes narrowed, and she peered through her glasses at the shiny comb. "It's very nice. Is it a gift?"

"Not really, no." Elizabeth touched her arm until the

old lady looked at her. Then mouthing each word with great exaggeration, she said slowly, "Is this your comb?"

Henrietta frowned. "Yes, I have a comb."

"But is this one yours?"

Still faced with the blank look, Elizabeth pointed to the comb, then Henrietta's hair, then at Henrietta herself. "Yours?"

"Oh, no." Henrietta shook her head and once more a gray hair or two drifted on the wind. "No, it's not mine. Never owned anything that fancy in me entire life."

Elizabeth sighed, then mouthed, "When will Charlie be coming down again?"

Henrietta put her hand up to her ear. "Eh?"

"Charlie," Elizabeth yelled. "When is he coming down again?"

"What? Sorry, your ladyship. Can't hear a word you're saying."

Giving up, Elizabeth smiled and nodded. She'd just have to keep a watch out for the errant grandson. Maybe a word or two in the bartender's ear at the Tudor Arms would help. Alfie had helped her out before once or twice. She could ask him to ring her if he saw Charlie come in.

Henrietta was chatting about the weeds along the garden path. "Look," she said, pointing at a clump of dandelions, "they'll be all over the garden if I don't get them pulled. Still, when I've left, it will be up to the new tenant to take care of them, won't it."

Elizabeth glanced at the weeds, and wondered if Henrietta had decided on a date to move out. She didn't feel like attempting to ask her. She was tired of shouting to make herself understood.

The dandelions straggled across the path, limp and bedraggled now that the cool night air had taken the stuffing out of them. Elizabeth noticed a couple of Henrietta's gray hairs caught in the spiky leaves. Seeing them triggered a memory of something that she couldn't quite put her finger on.

"Can I get you a cup of tea, Lady Elizabeth?" Henrietta asked, as she led Elizabeth up the path to the gate. "It won't take me a minute to put the kettle on."

Elizabeth shook her head. "No, thank you, Henrietta. I have some errands to run."

The elderly widow must have understood, as she said cheerfully, "Next time, then. I'll keep watch from my window so I can see you arrive. I spend most of my day there. I hate to miss anything. I see a lot from that window. I can watch the kiddies going to school, and the postman bringing me a letter from Charlie, and lots of people ride their bikes and wave as they go by."

"That's nice," Elizabeth murmured, forgetting that Henrietta couldn't hear her. She was thinking about something else. Something that had been bothering her for the past week. Something other than the hairs in the weeds. Something much more significant.

"I have to go," she said sharply. "I'll stop by again soon." She didn't wait to see if Henrietta had understood. She was in far too much of a hurry.

The engine of her motorcycle roared as she jumped on the kick start, disturbing the quiet peace of the countryside. Heedless of the gravel her spinning wheels kicked up, she shot out of the little lane and headed back down the coast road toward the church. She knew now why the hairs in the weeds had reminded her of something. Maybe that was what had triggered the rest of it. A lot of things were falling into place. Things she should have realized some time ago.

Cursing herself for being so incredibly dense, she roared up the hill to the church.

Before calling on the vicar, she walked once more around to the back of the church, and crouched down in front of the ground-level window. There were still hairs attached to the dry, splintered frame. Being careful not to dislodge them, Elizabeth peered through the dusty windowpane.

Obviously she was looking into the basement of the church, but it was far too dark to see much except for a few dark shapes covered by tarpaulins. She climbed to her feet. It was time to talk to the vicar once more.

The reverend answered the door to her knock, and invited her into his tiny parlor. "Would you like a cup of tea, Lady Elizabeth?" he asked her, as she unwound the scarf from her head. "I still have one in the pot. Deirdre made it for me before she left to go shopping. I was just on my way to the barber's. It's been so long since I had my hair cut, I'll very likely be mistaken for my wife if I don't see to it soon."

"Actually, Vicar, I just stopped by to ask you a question." Elizabeth hesitated. "Though a cup of tea does sound rather good right now."

"I won't take a minute. Sugar?"

"Two lumps, please, if you can spare some."

"Of course." The reverend waved her to a chair. "Make yourself comfortable."

She sat down, wondering how best to phrase the question she needed to ask. She didn't want to alarm the vicar unnecessarily, but if what she surmised was actually true, she would need his help.

He returned in record time and handed her the cup and saucer. "I won't join you this time. Two cups in one morning are more than enough for me."

She laughed to be polite and took a sip of the tea, then put the cup and saucer down on the wide arm of the chair. "Vicar, I was wondering, what do you keep in the basement of the church?"

He raised his eyebrows. "Keep? I don't keep anything down there, your ladyship. Well, some old records, I suppose. A couple of statues. Both broken, of course. They lost their heads when the oak tree came through the roof during that windstorm we had two years back. That's about it."

"And that's all?"

He sat down on a chair opposite her frowned. "To be honest, I don't exactly remember what's down there. No one's been down to the basement in more than five years. We kind of let things go down there for a while, then it got to the point when neither Deirdre nor I cared to venture down there."

Elizabeth took another sip of her tea. "Any particular reason?" she asked, as she replaced the cup in its saucer.

"Well, to be perfectly honest . . ." The vicar dropped his voice as if he were imparting a dreadful secret. "I'm afraid of rats, and my wife is afraid of dirt."

Suspecting he was poking fun at her, Elizabeth smiled. "So you've not been down to the basement in the last five years."

"That's right." The vicar narrowed his eyes. "Why do you ask?"

"What about the window in the basement?"

"There's a window? Well, yes, I suppose there must be. What about it?"

"Reverend," Elizabeth said, rising to her feet, "I wonder if you'd mind accompanying me to the church basement right now."

"Now?" The vicar sent a harried glance at the grandfather clock solemnly ticking away in the corner of the room. "Well, I was going to get my hair cut—"

"It *is* rather important."

"Oh, very well, your ladyship. If you insist. Though I must confess, I can't imagine why you would want to go down there. The last time I looked, it was damp, full of cobwebs, and crawling with all kinds of nasty things. Not the sort of place a lady such as yourself would want to be." He peered at her. "Not thinking of using it for some kind of meeting, were you? I can assure you, it's far too cold—"

"I'll explain when we get down there." Elizabeth crossed her fingers in the hope that her suspicions would prove to be justified, otherwise she would have a great deal of explaining to do.

CHAPTER
❈ 16 ❈

The vicar nodded, though obviously still mystified. "Just give me a minute to fetch my coat." He ambled over to the door. "Can't imagine why everyone seems so interested in my church basement all of a sudden."

"Everyone?" Elizabeth repeated sharply.

The vicar opened the door and without looking at her mumbled, "Oh, you're not the only one to ask me about that basement. I just don't understand it."

He disappeared before she could ask him who else had asked about the basement. By the time he returned, she decided to hold the question until she'd satisfied herself that her assumptions about the place were correct.

Walking by his side across the gravel courtyard to the church, she listened to him chatter on about the badly needed repairs to the roof, while part of her mind went over everything she had learned during the past few days. The more she thought about it, the more certain she was, and by the time the vicar had reached the door of the church, she was in a fever of impatience to find out if her deductions were correct.

The reverend led the way down the chilly hall between the vestibule and the dressing room where the choirboys changed into their angelic-looking gowns. Just beyond that he paused at a heavy door banded in steel and hesitated with a hand on the thick latch. "Are you quite sure you want to do this?" he asked, obviously hoping she'd changed her mind.

"Quite sure," Elizabeth assured him. Now that she'd come this far, she wasn't about to turn back.

"Very well." The reverend withdrew a ring of keys from his pocket and selected the only rusted one on the chain. He had to struggle to get it to turn in the lock, but finally, with a loud groan and an ugly creaking sound, the door swung open on its corroded hinges. "It's been so long since any of us have used this door," he muttered. "It's a miracle I managed to budge it at all."

Elizabeth glanced apprehensively at the steep stairs descending into the dark hole of the basement.

"I'll lead the way," the vicar announced, producing a torch from his pocket. "These steps can be somewhat tricky, your ladyship, so please be careful."

The narrow beam swept the wall on the left, then roamed over the handrail on the right to reveal part of the gloomy, cavernous room before swinging back to the stairs.

"Hold on tight as you go down," the vicar warned.

Elizabeth needed no urging on that point. She gripped the iron handrail, thankful for her leather gloves as she eyed the patches of rust and decay.

The vicar chattered cheerily as he descended one slow step at a time. Elizabeth couldn't tell if he was attempting to keep up her spirits or his own. Gingerly she followed him, being careful not to catch the heels of her sensible shoes on the edge of the uneven steps.

The church had been built several centuries earlier, and the stone staircase had been worn down by generations of feet. She tried not to think about the possibility of ghosts as she stepped down behind the stooped figure of the vicar.

Martin's rambling about seeing the ghost of her father in the great hall was giving her strange ideas. Impatient with herself, she concentrated on the more concrete possibilities that might lie ahead.

At long last she reached the bottom step and then the firm, flat stone floor of the basement. The reverend had been right about the cold. It rose from the floor and seeped from every wall in a chilling mass of foul, damp air.

As the beam from the vicar's torch roamed over the spacious room, a scuttling sound made her blood run cold. As if reading her thoughts, he said abruptly, "Well, I assume you've seen enough. Shall we go back to civilization?"

Shivering as the cold penetrated her thick coat, Elizabeth said quickly, "Not just yet. I'd like to see what's over by the window."

"My dear lady," the vicar murmured, "there's nothing over there but cobwebs, mold, and more than likely a hungry rat or two."

"Then perhaps you wouldn't mind telling me what lies under all those tarpaulins?"

The beam moved in her direction. "Which tarpaulins are you talking about?"

"The ones by the window." Elizabeth stepped past him and gestured at the far end of the room, where the small, square window allowed a murky shaft of light to penetrate the gloom. "Those tarpaulins, over there."

The beam followed the direction of her hand, but couldn't reach that far. Muttering under his breath, the vicar moved forward. The wide swath of light cut through the dark shadows, then rested on the tall, irregular shapes Elizabeth had spotted through the window.

"Bless my soul!" The vicar halted, staring at the shrouded objects. "I have no idea what they could be. I certainly don't remember seeing them here when I was down here last. Of course, that was more than five years ago, and my memory isn't what it used to be."

"Then perhaps we should refresh it, Vicar." Elizabeth walked bravely down the length of the beam and grasped one end of a tarpaulin. The pool of light brightened as the vicar came up behind her. With one swift tug the heavy cover slid to the ground.

She let out her breath in triumph. Clearly visible in the beam of the light the letters on the stack of crates could easily be read. UNITED STATES GOVERNMENT IS-SUE.

"Oh, my," the vicar said, sounding breathless. "How in the world did that get here?"

For answer, Elizabeth reached up and pushed on the window. It opened out easily, on well-oiled hinges.

The reverend gasped. "Goodness gracious. Someone came in through the window?"

"That's what I think." Elizabeth closed the window again. "There must have been two of them. One inside, to take the crates from the other person who handed them through the window. Probably in the middle of the night. Any footprints on the paved path outside would be covered up by other people walking by, or washed away in the rain. It would have been easy to carry the crates up the path from the lane, where the lorry was most likely parked, out of sight from the coast road. The perfect place to store stolen goods from the American base."

"Yes, I should say it is." The reverend's face looked worried in the glow from the torch. "Do you think this has something to do with the murder of that young American in the bell tower?"

"I'm almost certain of it." Elizabeth pulled the collar

of her coat closer around her neck. "Vicar, do you think you could keep all this to yourself for a little while? I need to talk to someone before we report to the authorities. If anyone else hears about this in the meantime, the culprits could get away, and I'm sure you wouldn't want that."

"Oh, no, not at all." The vicar directed the light beam over the other tarpaulins. "There does seem to be rather a lot here. Do you think they'll come back for it?"

"I'm sure they plan to, just as soon as the guards move out of the bell tower. I imagine they are just waiting for that to happen."

A look of alarm crossed his face. "That's tomorrow. The guard told me tomorrow was his last day."

"Then we have to move fast." Elizabeth started for the steps. "Please, Vicar, not a word."

"You have my solemn oath on that, your ladyship. Not a word. Not even to Deirdre."

Satisfied, Elizabeth started back to the vicarage to retrieve her scarf. "By the way, Vicar," she said, as they retraced their steps, "who else was it asking about the basement recently?"

"It was that nice little old widow, Henrietta Jones." The vicar stopped short. "Good Lord, you surely don't think *she* was the one crawling in and out of that window, do you?"

Her suspicion confirmed, Elizabeth laughed. "Of course not. Though she's certainly slim enough, at her age the feat would be quite extraordinary. Not to mention her rheumatism. Don't worry about it, Vicar. I'm sure we'll get it all sorted out by tomorrow."

She headed back to the Manor House, her mind working out what she needed to do. First, she must talk to Earl. She would need his help if she wanted to bring this case to a positive conclusion. If all went well, she might just possibly know the identity of Kenny Morris's killer by tomorrow.

Elizabeth had to wait until after the dinner hour before the American officers finally pulled into the courtyard in their jeeps. Having kept watch for an anxious hour or two, Elizabeth abandoned protocol and wasted no time in hurrying along the great hall to catch Earl before he retired to his room.

Conscious of the curious glances from the other officers, she caught his arm the second he strode through the door. "I wonder if I could have a word with you," she announced, much to the unmasked interest of the burly American who barged in close behind him.

"Sure." Earl handed the briefcase he was carrying to his companion.

The officer took it with a smirk that made Elizabeth cringe. "How come you deserve special privileges?" he asked, giving Elizabeth a disrespectful and totally lascivious wink.

"Cut it out, Madison," Earl growled.

She should have sent Violet or Martin to summon him, Elizabeth thought belatedly. If her mother could see her fraternizing like this, she'd come back and haunt her, too. "I'm terribly sorry to bother you like this, Major Monroe," she said loudly, in a belated attempt to create a more appropriate image, "but I'm afraid that something has come up that needs your immediate attention."

His gaze sharpened. "Lead the way, Lady Elizabeth. I'm all yours."

She hurried back down the hallway, trying not to dwell on the context of his last statement.

He waited until they were out of earshot before demanding, "What's happened?"

She raised a cautioning finger to her lips. "I'll tell you when we get to the conservatory. How was your day?"

He seemed surprised by the abrupt change of topic, but answered readily enough. "Pretty good. I guess we gave the Jerries something to think about, and for once everyone came back in one piece."

She shivered, thinking about the news broadcasts on the wireless. Every time someone announced the latest figures of German planes shot down, she had to wonder how many British planes had been lost. Most of the time all they were told was that British losses were light. Whatever that meant. Even one plane down could not be considered "light" in her opinion.

She was glad to reach the cozy comfort of the conservatory. The blazing fire in the library fireplace had heated the adjoining wall, keeping the tiny conservatory snug and warm. The sherry decanter that Violet had brought up two hours ago still sat untouched by the divan, and she accepted Earl's offer to pour her a glass.

She waited until he had settled down in his favorite chair before saying warily, "This is becoming a nightly habit. I hope it's not causing any discomfort for you?"

His gaze met hers, amusement flickering across his face. "In what way?"

The question unsettled her. "Well, I suppose I meant the reaction of the other officers."

"Like just now, you mean?"

She dropped her gaze to her glass. "Yes. I don't want anyone to misunderstand our relationship."

She could almost feel the thick silence between them. After much too long a pause, Earl asked quietly, "What are you trying to tell me, Elizabeth?"

Distressed now, she hastened to reassure him. "Nothing, really. You know how people talk. I was concerned you might be put in an awkward position with your fellow officers."

He put the glass down on the table between them. "Are you telling me you're worried about your reputation?"

She snapped her chin up. "Actually, I was more concerned about yours."

To her immense relief, he grinned. "Well, that's quite a switch."

She smiled happily at him. "Yes, isn't it. Usually I'm the one worrying about appearances."

"Does this mean you've stopped worrying?"

"Well, I wouldn't go so far as to say that."

"I still have to call you Lady Elizabeth in public?"

"I'm afraid so."

He nodded. "That's what I thought."

"It's tradition, you know. People don't have much else to hang on to right now. They find it comforting to know that some things haven't changed."

He laced his fingers together and tucked them under his chin. "British people are sure interesting. Your history goes way, way back before ours, and all that time everyone has been fighting to the death to keep things the way they've always been."

"We're a proud nation. We are proud of what we've achieved and we don't want anyone or anything interfering in our way of life."

"I figured that. On the other hand, there's my country, still pretty much in its infancy compared to yours, and ever since America was born, everyone over there has been fighting to change things. Make it better, make it bigger, make it different."

"Ah, but then you Americans have never learned the art of contentment."

"I guess we associate contentment with a danger of becoming stagnant."

"That's the difference between us, I suppose." She sipped her sherry, enjoying the tangy fire of it sliding down her throat. After a moment she added, "It will always be there, won't it?"

"What will?"

"The difference between us."

"I guess so. America is made up of pioneers, adventurers, and rebels. We're a rough bunch compared to the genteel folks of Old England."

It was on the tip of her tongue to comment that it was

that very aura of raw energy that made Americans so exciting, but thought better of it.

"Anyway," Earl said, mercifully changing the subject, "what was it you wanted to tell me? Or was that just an excuse to enjoy some more of my scintillating company?"

She laughed, delighting in the ease with which she could indulge in this pleasant banter with him. "Probably a little of both, I must confess. I do, however, have some rather important news to tell you. You see, I found the missing supplies from the base."

Caught in the middle of a sip, he almost choked. He put down his glass and pulled a large handkerchief from his pocket with which he dabbed his mouth before exclaiming, in a rather melodramatic manner, Elizabeth thought, "You what?"

"I found the missing supplies."

"When? Where? How?"

Elizabeth sighed. "They are stacked in the basement at St. Matthew's."

"The church?"

"Yes. I found them there this afternoon."

"The minister is hiding stolen goods?"

"No, no. The reverend had no idea they were there. He hasn't been down there in more than five years. He had an awful job getting the door to open, since it had rusted shut, but—"

"Wait a minute. If he didn't put the stuff there, how did it get there?"

"Well, we assume it got there through the window. It's at ground level, and it would have been quite simple to hand the crates through there. They're not that large, after all. Though quite heavy, I suppose."

Earl appeared dazed by this revelation. "So, do you know who did put them there? Besides Kenny, I mean."

"Well, I think I do. But I'm going to need your help to prove it."

She quickly outlined her plan, impressing upon Earl the need to act quickly. "Once they move the supplies, it would be very difficult to prove anything."

"So we wait in the basement for them to turn up tomorrow night."

"And catch them red-handed, so to speak."

"But that still doesn't tell us who killed Kenny Morris."

"Well, it just might. I have to talk to Henrietta Jones one more time. I'll pop along there first thing in the morning."

"You really think she's involved in this?"

"Well, I do know that Henrietta isn't all she seems. I think she could be covering up for Charlie, after all. I have a theory about the rest of it, but I won't know until I talk to her again."

Earl shook his head. "I don't know. I don't like the thought of you going back there. If Charlie was Kenny's contact, he'll be in the village to pick up the stuff tomorrow. He could be at the cottage right now."

"I don't think so." Elizabeth stretched out her feet and wriggled her toes. "I didn't see any sign of a car in the lane, or any tire tracks. Which makes me think that Charlie will come down tomorrow to pick up the goods. He's going to need something bigger than a car to take all those boxes out of there, and there aren't that many places to hide a lorry. No, I think he'll wait until the middle of the night to drive into Sitting Marsh. By then your men will be waiting for him, and whomever else he brings to help him."

"You're that sure he'll turn up? If he turns out to be Kenny's killer, I can't figure why he'd risk coming back to the village."

"He has to come back." Elizabeth smiled. "He has a loose end to tie up."

"Which is?"

"Henrietta Jones. He has to come back for her. Even

if he has no real affection for her, he can't afford to leave a witness behind—a frail old lady who might just get upset enough with him to tell the police what she knows. I'm hoping he'll be greedy enough to take the last of the supplies with him."

"Well, I hope you're right." Earl still looked worried. "How do you figure on finding out if he's the killer?"

"I'm hoping Henrietta will tell me."

"Why would she do that?"

"Because," Elizabeth said slowly, "as I said, she's an old lady, and rather defenseless. I'm hoping I can shake her up enough for her to tell me the whole truth. I think she trusts me."

"That's an awful lot of hoping and surmising going on there."

Elizabeth shrugged. "It's all we have."

"You know the investigators might not go for it."

"Then I suppose we'll have to get George and Sid down there."

"Not a lot of brain power in those two."

"It's better than nothing."

Earl threw his hands up in defeat. "Okay, I'll talk to the investigators and get back to you tomorrow."

Elizabeth could tell he wasn't happy with her theories. She had to admit, they rested on a pretty weak foundation. "Thank you, Earl. I know a lot of what I've said is going on assumption, but I have a hunch about this and I just have to play it out."

"I still don't like the idea of you going over to that widow's place tomorrow."

"I'll be perfectly all right." She watched him rise, then got to her feet with some reluctance. How she hated to end these pleasant interludes. "I'll go down there right after breakfast, and then I'll be back around eleven. So you can call me any time after that."

"Okay, if you say so. Good night, Elizabeth."

"Good night, Earl. And thank you."

"Sure. I just hope I'm not gonna regret this."

She watched him leave, anxious now for the night to be over. She couldn't wait to get back to Henrietta's cottage and confirm what she suspected.

CHAPTER

❧ 17 ❧

The rain had returned the next morning when Elizabeth left the house. In spite of her goggles, which covered a large portion of her face, and the bright yellow waterproof fisherman's hat she'd dug out of an old chest, somehow the raindrops found their way down her neck to soak the collar of her blouse.

The mackintosh she wore parted enough for the rain to drench her skirt, and she was quite a sorry sight by the time she arrived at Henrietta's cottage.

Marching up the path, her feet squelching inside her wet boots, she made a mental note to shop for a good set of oilskins to wear on her motorcycle during the winter months. This was one of the rare times she wished she could afford a motorcar.

She glanced at the front window, but could see no sign of Henrietta behind the bedraggled window boxes.

The widow had to be in the back of the house in the kitchen.

Elizabeth paused for a second or two, then lifted the knocker and let it fall. After a moment of silence had passed, she rapped again, this time putting some force behind the metal knocker. The wind whistled and moaned around the house, slapping wet leaves against the porch walls and raising goose bumps on Elizabeth's arms.

She waited, her patience slipping away with each passing moment. Again she rapped, louder and louder, more and more insistent. When she still received no answer to her summons, she stepped down from the porch into the teeth of the wind.

Leaning into the fierce blast, she walked back down the path to the lane and studied the ground. Still no tire tracks. The mud stirred up by the rain would certainly have left tracks if anything heavier than a bicycle had parked there. Charlie couldn't have arrived already, unless Henrietta left by foot to meet him somewhere.

Anxious now that all her plans were doomed for failure, Elizabeth pushed her way between two very wet, very prickly bushes to get up close to the window. The living room was dark, and it was difficult to see. The room appeared to be empty. She pushed hard on the window, but it was securely latched.

Frustrated, she went back to the front door and rammed the knocker down as hard as it would go. The door flew open, taking her completely off guard.

Henrietta stood with one hand on the doorjamb and stared hard at her. She appeared to be extremely put out. Her gravelly voice could barely mask her irritation. "Lady Elizabeth, what the . . . what on earth are you doing out here in this dreadful weather?"

"Oh, thank goodness." Without waiting for an invitation, Elizabeth stepped through the door, into the unpleasant odor of the living room. "I was afraid something awful had happened to you." She vaguely heard the door closing behind her, but her attention was immediately caught by the three suitcases sitting in the middle of the living room.

"Such a terrible day to be out, and you on a motor-cycle. It must be important to bring you out on such a day." Henrietta walked past her heading toward the kitchen. "You'll have to excuse me, Lady Elizabeth. I was cleaning out my cupboards. Everything is in a bit of a mess, I'm afraid. I hope you will excuse me if I don't have time to talk."

"Henrietta . . ." Elizabeth darted forward and grasped the old woman by the arm. To her intense surprise, she distinctly felt a hard muscle contract under her fingers.

Cold with shock, she let go at once.

Henrietta turned to look at her, and Elizabeth instinctively backed away.

"I just wanted to ask if there was anything I could get for you from town today," she said quickly. "I had to pass by here and thought you might need something."

The widow studied her with eyes that had grown hard and cold. "I really am very busy, Lady Elizabeth, as I'm sure you must be. Please don't let me keep you."

Elizabeth backed up another step. "Very well. Perhaps another day. Please don't bother to see me out. I'll be quite all right."

With a curt nod, Henrietta spun around and disappeared into the kitchen.

Elizabeth stared after her. She had to know for sure. It could have been her imagination. On the other hand, if she was right, Henrietta could be in terrible danger.

Raising her voice only slightly, she said, "I see Charlie has arrived. When did he get here?"

The rough voice answered her from the kitchen. "Charlie's not here. He—" The words broke off, followed by an ominous silence.

Elizabeth silently congratulated herself. As she'd suspected, whoever that was in the kitchen, she wasn't deaf, and she wasn't Henrietta. Fascinated in spite of her mounting apprehension, Elizabeth waited for the old woman.

When she finally moved into the doorway, she didn't speak. She just stood there in the entrance to the kitchen, poised like a cat watching a bird, just waiting for her prey to make a move.

Too late, Elizabeth realized she'd made a mistake. She forced her frozen mind to work. The front door was still several feet behind her. If she could make it to the porch, she might have a chance. The thing to do was keep talking until she could ease close enough to make a dash for it. "You seemed to have recovered your hearing," she said, using much the same tone of voice with which she'd discuss the weather.

She wasn't terribly surprised when the old woman lifted her hand and pulled the gray wig from her head. The lank blond hair, sheared in a military cut, seemed incongruous above the face that had been powdered almost white and carefully painted with lines to resemble wrinkles.

"Charlie, I assume?" Elizabeth said, sliding her foot backward.

"Now how in the hell did you manage to work that one out, your ladyship?"

Charlie's voice was rich with sarcasm, and Elizabeth felt an intense flash of resentment. She raised her chin. "What have you done with your grandmother?

He uttered a scornful laugh. It wasn't a pleasant sound. "There ain't no bloody grandma, is there. Not so bloody clever after all, are you, your bleeding ladyship."

"I don't understand." Elizabeth drew her right foot level with her left. "Isn't Henrietta your grandmother? Then who is she? Whoever she is, I know she isn't really deaf." Very slowly, she slid her left foot behind her again.

"What makes you think she ain't, then?"

"The first day I came here, Henrietta said she was in the kitchen making some tea. I heard the kettle stop whistling as she took it off the stove, just before I knocked. Yet she answered the door almost immediately. She couldn't have seen me arrive if she was in the kitchen, so she must have heard me."

Charlie bared uneven teeth in a ghastly grin. "Got it all worked out then, have you?"

Elizabeth eased her foot backward again. "Well, I assume, if she's not your grandmother, then she must be your accomplice. I thought she was covering up for you because you were her only relative, but you were paying her to help you, weren't you. You stayed with her here in the cottage, and pretended to be her when you went out so that you could go anywhere in town without anyone knowing you were there. Everyone naturally thought you were Henrietta."

"Very good, your ladyship."

She winced at the derisive note in his voice.

"That's why the gray hairs were caught in the window frame. I knew Henrietta couldn't have climbed through there, but you could, dressed in her clothes and a wig, of course. It must have been you who dropped the comb."

"Bleeding fountain of information, ain't you." He took a step toward her, alarming her.

"So where is Henrietta now? Is she all right?"

Charlie ran his tongue over his lower lip. "Well now, that's where you got it all wrong. There ain't no bleeding Henrietta."

Elizabeth continued to stare at him, until finally he muttered something she didn't catch. Then in a perfect imitation of Henrietta's voice he said, "Charlie's been ever so good to me since my Albert died. Not many young men like him would bother with an old lady the way he does. Our Charlie has a heart of gold, bless him.

Comes down every now and again to see me, he does. He's a good boy, is our Charlie."

Now she understood. And with it, came the realization that maybe she was in more trouble than she'd bargained for. "So there never was a Henrietta. It was you all the time."

"Right. I'm surprised someone as brilliant as you're supposed to be didn't twig it from the start."

"And you killed Kenny," Elizabeth said flatly. Once more she drew her feet level, bringing her inches closer to the door. "There was no funeral, of course. You made the whole thing up. You supplied your own alibi. You were here that weekend, after all."

Charlie shrugged. "Had to tell you something, didn't I."

"So why did you kill Kenny?"

She managed to gain a few more inches, but Charlie had also moved forward a step. She tried to remember which side of the door the latch was on. It could mean the difference between life and death.

"Kenny got greedy. Lost all his money in a poker game and wanted to charge me more for the stuff." Charlie made a sound of disgust. "Said he'd quit if I didn't pay up. I couldn't let him do that, now, could I. I work for some pretty mean bruisers up there in the city. They'd have skinned me alive. I told him I'd blow the whistle on him if he quit. I didn't mean to kill him, but things got nasty and he pulled a knife. I didn't have no choice then, did I."

Elizabeth eased back another step. "Look, I'm sure if you plead self-defense, the courts will be lenient with you."

"Yeah, well, I'm not taking no chances on the judges." Charlie took another step toward her. "You should have left when you had the chance. But then, you always did talk too much."

Elizabeth bristled. "I beg your pardon—" Her words

broke off in a scream as Charlie produced a knife from his apron pocket. "Poor Henrietta," he said softly. "Off her rocker, she was. Stabbed the nice lady of the manor, then took off. Nobody will ever know what happened to her."

Elizabeth spun around and lunged for the door. It burst open as she reached it, cracking her knuckles so hard, the pain brought tears to her eyes. Through the mist she saw a tall man charge past her, and by the time she realized it was Earl, he had Charlie on the floor and was sitting on him.

"One move and I break your arm off," he snarled, as Charlie struggled beneath him.

She was about to ask him where on earth he'd come from when two men appeared in the doorway. "Looks like we got here just in time," Captain Johansen remarked.

Elizabeth couldn't agree more.

"You gave me one heck of a scare," Earl said later that afternoon, as he stooped to pick up a bright red ball from the grass. He drew back his arm and let fly, watching the ball as it curved gracefully through the air, chased by two pudgy, yapping puppies.

Elizabeth smiled at the sight of the two round furry bodies scrambling over each other. "I was a little unnerved myself," she admitted. "Thank goodness you arrived on the scene when you did. I was never more happy to see anyone in my life."

"In that case, I'll have to play rescuer more often."

Unsettled by the remark, she kept her gaze on the dogs. "I hope it won't be necessary in the future."

"Amen to that. I would never have forgiven myself if anything had happened to you." George had retrieved the ball and dropped it at Earl's feet. He hopped a couple of steps, then kicked it, sending it soaring across the lawn.

"You certainly wouldn't have been to blame," Elizabeth pointed out. "After all, you did warn me that Charlie might be there at the cottage."

"Yeah, but I also know that you don't pay much attention to warnings."

"A bad habit of mine. It was a mistake."

"Almost your last mistake."

The note of seriousness in his voice struck a chord. She sent him a quick glance, half afraid of what she'd see in his eyes. His face was as grave as his voice had been.

"What made you decide to follow me down to the cottage, anyway?"

He didn't answer right away. He crouched on his heels, his hand outstretched toward the puppies, who had abandoned the ball in favor of a pinecone. Finally he said quietly, "I don't really know. Just a hunch—a feeling, I guess, that you were walking into trouble. I couldn't settle down, so I left a message for the investigators to meet me there, and I checked out of the base. I was standing at the front door, trying to decide if I was making one big ass of myself when I heard you scream. Luckily the door wasn't locked. The doors in this country are thick enough to withstand a tank."

"They're built to keep out the cold." She watched the wind ruffle a lock of his hair and curled her fingers into her palm. "Thank you, Earl. You probably saved my life."

"Does that make you my slave or something?" He glanced up at her, his eyes crinkling at the edges.

She managed a light laugh. "You know the song . . . Rule Britannia and all that."

"Ah, yes . . . something about Britains never being slaves. Guess I'll just have to settle for friendship, then."

"That goes without saying."

He gave her one of those long looks that did unimaginable things to her stomach, then rose to his feet.

"Guess I'd better get back to the base before they miss me."

As always, she hated to see him go. "Thank you for being there for me. I hope I can repay the debt some-time—"

Her heart seemed to stop beating when he reached for her hand. He studied her fingers lying in his palm, while she did her best to breathe normally. "Elizabeth, I . . ."

She felt as if she were poised on the brink of a huge wave, waiting to see if it would carry her soaring to the beach, or dash her into the foaming waters.

"I have to go," he said at last.

She smiled, though her heart ached to know what it was he had been about to say. "You'll let me know how everything turns out?"

"You'll probably know before I do. The investigators will question Charlie, then, since he's a British civilian, release him to the custody of your constables to await trial."

She nodded, not trusting herself to speak.

He left her standing there, watching the empty drive-way long after the roar of his jeep had faded into the distance.

"I can't believe that Henrietta Jones was really her grandson dressed up as her," Violet remarked, as she served her version of a beef stew for supper that eve-ning. "I talked to her myself in the town and I never had an inkling she wasn't an old lady. He must have been very clever with makeup, that's all I can say."

"He was. I didn't realize it myself until I actually touched him." Elizabeth broke off a piece of bread and popped it into her mouth.

"Ugh!" Violet put a plate of the stew in front of Mar-tin, who sniffed cautiously at it, then wrinkled his nose. "You must have been horrified when you found out."

"I should have realized it earlier, when I remembered

that Henrietta had opened the door to me the first time I went there, even though she was in the kitchen when I knocked. I simply thought that she was covering for her grandson and had pretended to be deaf to avoid awkward questions. It was so easy for her . . . him to pretend he didn't understand what I was asking him."

Violet brought her own plate to the table and sat down. Martin hadn't begun to eat and she gave him a sharp look. "If you're not going to eat that," she said tartly, "there are two dogs here who'd love to gobble it up."

Martin sniffed. "No doubt, since it's more suitable for their palate than mine."

"Ungrateful bugger. Just think yourself lucky you're not living on roots and berries, like some poor devils."

"That would at least be nutritious." He picked up his spoon and collected some of the stew on the end of it. "What is in this, anyway? Something that passes for meat, I presume, but what are these little green things floating around in it?"

"Parsley," Violet snapped. "It's good for your bowels."

Martin blinked at her over his glasses. "There's nothing wrong with my bowels."

"There will be if you don't eat your blinking stew." Violet rolled her eyes at Elizabeth. "Drives me bonkers, he does."

Elizabeth smiled at Martin. "Eat your supper, Martin. You need to keep up your strength."

"Yes, madam." Obediently he dug the spoon into the stew, while Violet uttered an exaggerated sigh.

"So Charlie was the one giving Percy all that food from the base," she said, after giving Martin one last glare. "I did wonder how he got all that stuff. He's always had a few bits and pieces under the counter, but nothing like the amount he had there for a while. Still, when you get a chance to buy some extra on the side, you don't ask questions, do you."

"Which is exactly why Charlie could get away with it. I talked to George this afternoon, and he told me that Charlie was involved in a pretty big organization in London. Apparently the leaders hired small-time crooks and paid them a percentage to contact the American bases all over the country and set up black market deals with the Americans."

"Well, they won't be doing that no more, will they."

Elizabeth sighed. "No matter how many of those people get apprehended, there will always be more to take their place."

"Fortunes of war, I suppose. Some people will always make money out of it."

Even Percy. Elizabeth refrained from uttering the thought aloud. "Anyway, all the stolen goods were supposed to be shipped directly to London, but Charlie decided to do some extra business on the side and keep the profits for himself."

"So he was selling to other people besides Percy?"

Elizabeth nodded. "Bessie, for one. I imagine he was doing business in North Horsham as well. You see, Charlie is AWOL from the army. The real Henrietta died a few months ago, and Charlie never returned from his compassionate leave. Instead, he assumed her identity and leased the cottage in Sitting Marsh to avoid being picked up by the military police. Since he was supposed to be an elderly widow, he needed some kind of transportation back and forth to town. Which is why he started supplying Percy. I suppose it all ballooned from there."

"So Charlie never did have a flat in London?"

"No. He transported the goods to London, then returned immediately to Sitting Marsh."

"Pretty good disguise, if you ask me. I don't think anyone twigged it."

"We probably never would if things hadn't started to go wrong. First there was the cricket match, which meant Charlie had to move his stores out of the pavilion and find another place for them. Then when Kenny was killed, that complicated things even more."

Violet slurped the gravy on her spoon. "How did you know the crates were in the church basement?"

"I remembered seeing the gray hairs on the window frame and the ones caught on the silver comb. When I showed them to Marlene, she said the hair was in very poor condition. When I realized that Henrietta wasn't really deaf, and I thought she was covering up for Charlie, I started thinking about those hairs at the church and what Marlene had said. That's when I guessed that Charlie had dressed up as Henrietta and was actually wearing a wig when he moved the crates. That's where the hairs came from."

"Well, you were right about that, at least." ·

Elizabeth watched Violet take a piece of bread and wipe it around her plate. "It just didn't occur to me that I'd been talking to Charlie all that time, instead of Henrietta. When she complained about her rheumatics, that was the pain from the knife wound Charlie had received in the fight with Kenny. That alone will be enough to convict him."

"Just goes to show, you never know who you're talking to these days."

"That's exactly what I say," Martin announced, having remained unusually quiet throughout the conversation. "I was talking to the master this morning, and before I realized it, he'd disappeared and I was talking to the suit of armor instead."

Violet looked at Elizabeth and jerked her chin in Martin's direction. "Gets worse, he does."

"Anyway," Elizabeth said, ignoring the comment, "luckily for me, Earl decided to follow up on a hunch that I could be in danger. If he hadn't, I might well have shared the same fate as Kenny Morris."

Violet huffed out her breath. "Seems to me you and that major are getting really friendly lately."

Elizabeth cast her gaze down at her plate. Irritated to feel her cheeks growing warm, she muttered, "One has to be pleasant to the American officers. They are our guests, after all."

"Uninvited guests," Violet reminded her. She reached across the table and laid a bony hand on Elizabeth's arm. "I don't want to see you get hurt again, Lizzie. You've been through so much already with that rotter Harry. Just be careful what you're doing, all right?"

Elizabeth patted the slender fingers. "Don't worry, Violet, there's nothing like that between the major and me. In the first place, I'm much too sensible to get involved with another man, and in the second place, the major has a wife and two children waiting for him in America."

"Well, all right then." Apparently satisfied she'd done her duty, Violet sat back. "Then thank Gawd he was there. I just hope this will be a lesson to you, Lizzie, and you'll keep your nose out of any nasty business from now on. You have enough to do running this estate, without trying to do Sid and George's job for them as well."

"Let us hope there will never be a need for me to get involved in murder again."

"Too right. You've had a lucky escape. Now all we have to worry about is who will win that baseball game with the Yanks."

Martin coughed. "And what, pray, is a baseball?"

Violet sighed. "You tell him. You've got more patience than I have."

"It's a game like rounders," Elizabeth said. "You hit the ball and run around a square to get home before the ball does."

Martin frowned. "I've never seen a ball run around a square before. Must be a special kind of ball."

"No, you silly old fool," Violet burst in. "The ball doesn't run around the square . . ."

Elizabeth sat back, content to listen to them bickering. Things were back to normal. Now she could pay attention to the repair bills, and the rents due, and the baseball game, and an occasional glass of sherry in the conservatory with Earl at her side. She had a lot to look forward to, and if she felt a pang of regret at the loss of excitement of a murder investigation, she refused to dwell on it. Knowing that she could bump into Earl Monroe at any given moment was all the excitement she needed.